SEE YOU LATER

By

Daniel Lorn

This is a work of fiction. Names, characters, businesses, places, events and incidences are either the products of the author's imagination or used in a fictitious manner. Any resemblance to actual persons, living or dead, or actual events, is purely coincidental.

See You Later
First Edition October 2020
Current Edition October 2022
Copyright © 2022 Daniel Lorn

All rights reserved. No portion of this book may be reproduced, copied, distributed or adapted in any way, except for certain activities permitted by applicable copyright laws, such as brief quotations in the context of a review or academic work. For permission to publish, distribute or otherwise reproduce this work, please contact the author at daniel.lorn@outlook.com.

We cannot forever ignore the terrifying monsters that squirm around in the darkness of our connected minds.

DANIEL LORN

PROLOGUE

Nothing could have ever prepared me for the horrifying events that have unfolded over the past few days. Everything seems to have happened so suddenly, but I guess, not without warning. If only I had acted with more trepidation, I might have had a chance to escape the manifestations of my past.

Something has come to claim my soul. It is in no hurry to consume me, and I can feel its presence bearing upon me, nearing closer with every desperate breath I take. I also know the truth of what stalks me from the shadows. I know this because I had sealed this fate many years ago. You see, death is not the end; it is but a catalyst to enter the realms forbidden to tread as a mortal.

Beyond the shadows of physical exploration lies an inconceivable domain—a world we only touch the boundaries of during our worst nightmares. Maybe if I allow myself to fall asleep again, I will wake up and realise that's what all this was; just a nightmare. One that was close to revealing its terrifying climax. Or maybe insanity will even become my saviour.

Paralysed on a bed where I will soon struggle for my last breath, all I can do is wait. Every nerve fibre in my body pulsates unbearably in reflex to the sensation of unseen creatures desperate to sear my flesh. My energy levels are fading fast, and any fight within me has long surrendered to the imminent darkness and the things which pulsate within. Even now, I can hear the faint echo of their unfathomable utterances. This cacophony serves as a stark warning. From the decaying fissures hidden beyond reality, these unclean entities will soon burst through the ripped lungs of my walls to unleash their final, unrelenting fury upon me. And even though the concept of witnessing these abominations petrifies me, death alone would be a welcome respite from this torture.

I am compelled to close my eyes. Maybe my own mortality will feast on me as I sleep and save me from their writhing and vile clutches. As the final strands of consciousness escape me, the beginning of this ordeal begins to play out in my mind like a movie.

My eyelids slowly drape over my tired eyes.

And finally…Sleep.

CHAPTER 1

1988

I grew up in Pollok, a suburb in southwest Glasgow. Pollok, at the time, was a housing estate filled predominantly with three and four-story tenement buildings. My Grandmother told me once that the estate was built during the second world war, as the inner city was becoming increasingly overcrowded. Each gathering of grey-washed brick buildings formed separate communities where everyone knew their neighbour. Children would race outside to play on the equally grey streets before the warm glow of the streetlamps indicated it was time to head home.

With no cellphones or accessible internet in those days, physical interaction with others was commonplace and social connections, good or bad, were unavoidable. Consequently, just as naturally as fallen rain joins the steady flow of a river, I found myself sharing the company of a remarkably odd-looking bunch—a term coined by Josh on behalf of his awkward height and narrow shoulders.

Josh was a self-confessed nerd. Rather than head into the great outdoors, he preferred to stay home playing chess or Dungeons and Dragons. He occasionally ventured outside, but only if he really had to and only if the sun was out, as his glasses tended to steam up in the cold.

Then there was Shaun. He always dreamed of being a policeman and used to practice daily by marching around, yelling at people to stay off the grass and trying to break up any playground fights. In contrast to Josh, Shaun was short and stocky with a black helmet of hair, which was always heavily glazed with gel. He had a bit of a complex about his appearance and always made that extra effort.

Shaun was best pals with Todd, the youngest member of our group. Todd was slim and frail with pale, thin, almost white hair. He always complained about his 'bad knees', which he liked to blame as an excuse for his paltry height and inability to partake in any sport. He was also obsessed with superheroes.

As social misfits, we had plenty in common, but it wasn't

until Jack arrived in primary three that I understood the term 'best friend'. Jack was given the empty seat next to me in class on his first day, and it soon became clear we had plenty in common. With light brown hair and huge dimples on our cheeks when we smiled, we often got mistaken for brothers. We were also the same height, although Jack appeared much older and was already showing a slightly more athletic frame than many. He also had a natural air of confidence and no trouble speaking to girls. However, the one thing that genuinely bonded us was our unhealthy appetite for horror movies. I fondly recall us sneaking out of my room during our regular weekend sleepovers when my parents were in bed. Once in front of the TV, we would stay awake for hours watching the latest scary movie we had acquired. Very quickly, we became best buddies, thick as thieves.

I resided on the top floor of a four-story tenement flat with my mother and father. Josh and Shaun lived with their respective families around the corner in a more pleasant cul-de-sac marginally calmer than my bustling street. Todd's mother had recently moved with him to a small house with a view of Crookston Castle, which sat atop a hill overlooking much of the surrounding area. Jack, on the other hand, stayed deep in the centre of one of the rougher council schemes with his mother. A place where muggings and stabbings were unfortunately commonplace.

Our primary school served many of the locals from its dominant position in the centre of a vast green field beside Rosshall Park. The park's main body wrapped its way around the central estate. It was our favoured place to explore during the holidays. We knew every inch of the area entirely. Sprightly green strips of treeline and bushes concealed secret granite pathways, and a refreshing scent from the evergreen trees sweetened the air. In the middle was a large patch of lush green grass leading down to a small pond thriving with tadpoles and floating lilypads. The enclosure was bordered on all sides by giant redwood trees that dominated the horizon. A partially concealed stone path was accessible at the right-hand side of the pond, and a low wall of rocks flanked both sides of the passageway through the creeping trees and bushes onto a series of scattered Pulhamite structures. The trail looped around to the other side of the pond to meet commanding chestnut trees that towered above thick bushes awash with yellow and green leaves. Vibrant with the sounds of wildlife lurking just out of sight, it was a perfect place to act out childhood fantasies, usually involving monsters or ghouls following us home. In the daylight, its embrace was welcoming, bright and joyful, but at night, it immediately transformed into a place filled with hidden eyes and reaching hands.

Even with my and Jack's invested love of the macabre, neither of us imagined the events that would soon unfold. Events which would end up haunting us for the rest of our lives.

It was the summer of 1988 when something real and terrifying followed me home from that park. We had been out trying to squeeze in one more adventure to mark secondary school's commencement and as a farewell to my best friend. Jack was leaving for England due to some difficulty his mother was in, and whilst he seemed in high spirits, we all knew that he was deeply saddened to leave. All of us would miss him, especially me.

The darkness was starting to creep in on the long summer day, and a grey cloud loomed above us with the threat of a forthcoming downpour. The smell of rain carried in the atmosphere as we headed towards the stone bridge that reached across to my estate. As we waited for the moonlight to arrive, we took turns throwing our collected pinecones into the frothing river. Empty cans of beer and wine bottles glistened under the surface as each pinecone splashed into the water and resurfaced to glide onwards with the flow.

As we leaned over the bridge railings, a murmured hissing filled the sky above. Scatterings of rain danced over the river and tapped on the tree tops as the clouds finally wept. We were just about to head home when I became strangely compelled to glance back along the path by the river. Through the rain, I could see a tall figure staggering along the track. Jack and I wasted no time scaring Josh, Shaun, and Todd into a fast retreat by pretending that it was an evil monster coming to get them.

Jack and I remained on the bridge as our friends swiftly ran to the rain-hazed glow of the estate. I decided it would be a brilliant idea to hide in the bushes beside the river and frighten our approaching victim out of his wits. Jack agreed with this plan, and we quickly found the perfect location for our attack behind an old chestnut tree that served as a decent rain shelter.

As he neared us, we kept completely still. Excitement burning in our bellies, we listened to the hypnotic chant of the river splashing underneath the hammering rainfall. My attention became arrested by the sound of soft and staggering footsteps gaining on our position, and I peeked around the tree to realise the target for our prank was none other than a man called Old Charlie. Charlie was undoubtedly on his way back from drinking whiskey at the local working man's club. He wore a dark raincoat, and his face was a blurred shadow, but I knew it to be him.

Charlie occupied a ground-floor flat directly opposite the park. Our only interaction with him was when he screamed and shouted at us for kicking a football into his beloved garden. He was a generally reticent old guy with whom no one bothered. There were rumours that he had killed many people during the war, which was why he wished to be left alone. My Gran always told me to keep out of his way, mumbling something about him being heard screaming frantically throughout the night, usually if he had been drinking. When I tried to enquire further, she would mutter, "The less you know about that man, the better."

We had never seen Charlie with any companions. It was unlikely he had any family remaining, as he must have been at least eighty and, according to my Gran, had no children. His regular trips to the pub and local shops were the only times he appeared to leave the house.

As Charlie bundled forward, it was clear to Jack and me that he was more inebriated than we had initially considered. He staggered forwards under the haze of rain, repeatedly cursing under his breath as he struggled to travel in a straight line. Unexpectedly, Charlie abruptly braced up dead straight and stood completely still as though startled, his silhouette fizzing under the rain that bled down between the gaps in the forest canopy. After a short moment, he began slowly shuffling forward again, a bit more stealthily this time.

"This will be great," I whispered to Jack; "the old guy will shit himself sober."

We waited a few seconds, then pounced before him to unleash a wild, bone-curdling scream.

Charlie wasn't prepared for this at all. The whites of his eyes glistened under the sparse moonlight glare as he uttered a raspy groan and hopped onto one foot. Next, he flopped over the fence that separated the path and river, rolling down the short embankment and coming to rest amongst the reeds.

We observed in dismay as Charlie sloped backwards into the undergrowth while clutching his chest with both hands. Jack and I froze in horror at what we were witnessing, whilst Charlie's glowing orbs fixated on our terrified expressions. He glared at us with petrified anguish for what seemed like an eternity until his eyes rolled back in his head. The thick reeds swallowed him as he slumped helplessly into their eager embrace, and the rain tapped furiously over the stalks which entombed him as though giant nails were being hammered into a coffin lid. At that moment, it was as if nature had consumed him like a spider feasting on a fly trapped in its web.

Crying with tears that washed away in the rain and our little hearts pumping like steam trains, Jack and I raced down the path and over the bridge. Once on the other side, we separated and headed to the refuge of our homes. On the way, Jack pleaded with me not to speak to anyone of this for fear of the trouble we would face, and I agreed.

I did not leave the house for the remainder of the week. I was much too terrified to face anyone, probably out of guilt for what we had just done.

Jack moved away as planned the very next day.

2004

I always relished the walk into the city from my humble abode.

Away from the hustle and bustle of the main streets, it was perfect for me. A mixture of qualified professionals and medical students studying at the local university also called this place home. I resided in the tallest of two modern buildings that reached up to pierce the canopy of blue sky. My apartment was second top, commanding a view over the adjacent park and onto the smoky grey city centre beyond. In contrast to the more populated parts of Glasgow, it was marginally more peaceful and restrained.

As I escaped the building's cool shadow, a sharp glaze of sunlight leapt into the brief gap in the shade. Its bright warmth made me narrow my eyes as I crossed the road towards the park directly in front of me. A wide path stretched under my feet and through the park gates, revealing an area proudly blossoming into the season. Flowers littered lush banks of deep green grass, and the whisper of birdsong filled the sycamore trees. Underfoot, fallen cherry blossom sprinklings led the way forwards. The azure above was like a dome of plasma blue with only a scattering of clouds basking under the gleaming disc of the sun. Spring had indeed arrived in Glasgow.

Although I finished school with minimal academic potential, my flare for computers allowed me to secure a job working as an online consultant for IT support. The money wasn't great, but it was flexible, allowing me to work hours that suited me. I wasn't by any means money-driven. As long as I had enough cash to pay the bills and order takeaway now and again, I was content. I lived a relatively modest existence, enjoying the quiet splendour of my own company, and feeling much more comfortable far away from others.

The slow drum of lawnmowers and the fizzing of sprinklers accompanied me on my stroll past scatterings of animated people sharing a laugh whilst quenching their thirst with a cold drink. Further along, several kids chased each other with excitement and verve through the glistening and colourful gardens. In the playpark, proud parents pushed their giggling toddlers on the swings and roundabouts whilst others sat lazily on benches to embrace the rare warmth with an ice cream cone. Several fitness enthusiasts swept past me with their faces red, music buzzing from their large headphones as their heavy feet pounded on the hot granite path.

Bright yellow and orange flowers filled gaps in the neatly cut grass, which had left its warming scent in the air.

Commuters avoiding the traffic cycled through the park, occasionally ringing their bells to communicate their approach to the occasional dog walkers and tourists who filtered in from each direction. Intoxicating aromas of citrus blossoms and pink jasmine filled my lungs, and I sighed with bliss at the calm and serenity of my surroundings.

As a creature of routine, I was very much set in my ways. It was easier that way. Sure, I often got jealous when witnessing other people's happiness, but I had convinced myself over time that it was best for me to live a more sheltered life. Certain events from my past had caused me to fall out of sync with any sense of social normality. Consequently, my brain had become conditioned to remain distant from many of life's ordinary interactions. As the world and its inhabitants celebrated existence around me, I would observe from the background of life's canvas, tuned out of any connection to its tapestry.

If any anxieties stirred within me, I had hard-wired a protective response, a reflex, to lock them away in the corner of my mind, along with other memories I wanted to forget. I wasn't overly happy, but I was at least content within my little bubble. My safe zone.

However, there was still an ingrained and unsatisfied need

within me that threatened to tip the balance of my self-control. I often struggled to suppress a longing—an inherent human need for marriage, children, or any meaningful relationship, to be honest. The only problem was that I could never open up to anyone about my history, nor could I see myself spending enough time with another person without letting my guard down. The protective shroud I had forged allowed me to at least semi-exist whilst simultaneously evading the scars from my past. My silhouette probably cast less of a shadow than those basking in the sun without a care.

The path led me through a break in the trees to reveal an old victorian stone bridge reaching over the river towards the Art Gallery and Museum just a few hundred metres in the distance. A marker for the park exit onto the main street. The sun warmed my skin as the trees furrowed away, and my imagination sneaked back to the smaller bridge from Pollok, where we used to throw pinecones in the river, albeit this bridge was much more extensive.

Just as the memory flashed in, it began to discolour with threat, and I quickly disarmed the invasion on my tranquil thoughts. Something I had conditioned myself to do almost subconsciously by reminiscing about the fonder memories of growing up and ensuring that my day had routine and direction. It was becoming easier the older I got to switch off the intrusion of painful recollections. I knew it wasn't a healthy way to be. Still, it worked for me, and soon I would be able to reminisce some of the good times when I caught up with my old friends. A stirring of excitement reminded me how much I was looking forward to catching up with the guys for our annual reunion—my only real connection to society. Whereas our get-togethers were occurring less and less often the older we got, it was still great to see the old faces. Not all of the old faces, of course. Josh, Shaun and Todd were the only contacts I had retained since school, and that was fine with me.

The songs and scents of spring dimmed as I crossed the bridge, and the warm embrace of the park faded behind me as I stepped onto the main street, which served as an artery flowing through the city's heart. A subtle din of popular songs sprayed out of the various drinking establishments' open windows, orchestrating the desired vibe for the evening. Vibrations from the city traffic rumbled under my feet as I stepped onto the tarmac road, which felt soft under my tread. University students dominated the local libraries and coffee shops overlooking the main road. Others chose to frequent the many modern local bars within stunning old-fashioned victorian buildings of striking red and deep brown painted sandstone.

It was almost six o'clock, and there was still no sign of the sun fading as I entered the bar to the cool, welcoming breeze of air conditioning fanning the threshold. Taking a deep breath to steady my nerve, I quickly put on my mask of normality before heading to the guys who were already seated in the same places as always.

Josh sat to the left of my vacant chair. He still considered himself a nerd, but a nerd who was married with two children to a teacher. His hairline was slightly receding, but he had filled out into his 6ft chassis and always wore a checkered shirt, chinos and a blue sports jacket. Josh still needed to wear glasses but never in public, preferring to narrow his eyes to focus instead. He had a great job as the lead consultant of a famous software firm, and although he didn't like to discuss it, it was apparent he was pretty well off. Next to Josh and across the table, Shaun bustled full of vigour, absolutely transfixed within the moment. Shaun wasn't as stocky anymore but was much more athletic. He worked as a personal trainer in one of the 24-hour gyms nearby. Unfortunately, he failed the entrance exam for the police but was studying hard for another try the following year. He wore his favourite black shirt and blue jeans, joking that it showed off his *buffness,* and still put too much gel on his now spiky hairstyle. Beside Shaun sat Todd in his two-piece suit and neatly styled blonde hair. Todd still tended to complain about his bad knees and blamed that for having become quite portly. He dressed in black because he said it was *slimming.* Todd had been diagnosed with autism and worked at a special needs centre for vulnerable children. He didn't drink or cope well in large crowds, but he was fine in the company of his friends and glowed with delight at having the old team back together again.

Indeed, a lot had changed, but the group was easily identifiable from childhood, apart from one extra person I hadn't expected to be there.

My heart skipped a beat for a moment, and I almost turned away to leave that place but instead, I felt my feet slow to a halt. My uneasy stare was fixated on this uninvited guest as the rising bellows within my chest threatened to make me keel over.

How long I stood there for, I do not recall. I do, however, remember my blood running cold as I met the gaze of my old friend Jack.

1988

A deep cold chill lingered within me long after I arrived home. It was as if I still carried the park's atmosphere on my clothing and skin—a fragmented reminder of what happened with Old Charlie. An open wound which refused to close. I tried settling my composure in the bedroom to avoid interacting with my parents. Desperate as I was to find shelter from the tangible sense of impending doom which obscured any safety my house once offered. Trying to switch off my nerve-shattered mind, I reached for my favourite book, but it wasn't long before I realised that the chill within my bones, which had lingered since the park, was unlikely to give me any respite.

The house seemed deprived of any habitual offering of protection. Even the cool air felt poised with the warning of a hidden entity whispering at me from behind the darkened windows. Recognising that sleep would not come easy, I decided it was time to try and steady my nerve. To quell the sensation of my heavy chest and my thumping heartbeat. My breath swirled in the air as I willed my body and mind to relax, but I couldn't manage to escape the overwhelming panic which filled my bones.

My heart thumped hard, constricting my chest in response to every sound. It was as though my subconscious mind was searching out a rational reason for the terror fouling my resolve. I shivered under my blanket as an overwhelming density of dread filtered through the gaps like deadly poison entering the bloodstream.

The fading chords of the ice cream van travelling further into the distance informed me it was almost ten o'clock, and usually, I would drift off in synchronisation with its melody. However, my senses were too fired up to embrace the sweet mercy of relaxation. It also didn't help that my parents added another layer to my anxiety by having one of their increasingly recurring arguments—noises such as shouting always served to make me very unnerved. Having listened to them yelling at each other over the years, I had developed a coping strategy which tended to work. With the remnants of the foul atmosphere from the park emblazed within my every fibre, I initially felt this to be a lost cause. However, after much perseverance, I steadied my breathing, allowing my body to relax its response to the external world. Eventually, I even managed to attain some distance from their shouts and the stifling atmosphere in my bedroom.

Closing my eyes tightly, I focussed on the cloak of darkness behind my eyelids and watched it swirl and transform before me. At the same time, I slowed my breathing further and imagined the black void to be thickening and lightening in density, in synchronisation with each gentle breath I took. As I breathed gently out, it felt like I was moving towards a pitch-black hole—an opening within the fabric of nature, which had materialised amongst the fizzing void.

The songs of awakened reality continued to stir, but their sounds affected me less with each deep breath in and slow, relaxed breath out. The dark circle I had manifested became larger and changed in density as it flooded through me. My feet began to tingle at the soles, which always proceeded full closure on the suppressing noises, just before I went limp and entered a dream-like state. I was then flying just above the ground of a barren landscape, fleeing the clamour of my parents' angered interactions. Even the creeping sense of threat that had followed me since the park failed to match my pace. As I had conditioned myself to do over the years, I completely tuned out the negative frequency of my parent's altercation. I soared further away as their words dimmed to nothing more than a dull buzzing, and I continued drifting towards another hole ripped into the ground, which I knew to lead into a tunnel network, just big enough to allow me access. Once inside those tunnels, I raced around them until the sounds completely faded from my thoughts. The labyrinth was endless, but just like in the park where my friends and I would chase each other around, I had learned the route which led to my destination.

At a specific juncture within the network, a great blanket of light would wash over me, and I would awaken none the wiser the next day, refreshed and well-rested. But on that particular occasion, something interrupted the process, and I had my very first episode of sleep paralysis.

It was an experience that terrified me profoundly but was strangely familiar at the very same time. Alone and with little more than my thoughts for company, I tried to force my heavy limbs to move, but they stubbornly denied the commands of my mind. It doesn't take much for one's imagination to explore all that the night has to offer, and it wasn't long before I noticed a sinister sensation which chilled me to the marrow of my bones. It was as if creeping fingers from somewhere unseen were trying to burrow their way into existence. A pungent smell of wet weeds and faeces entered my gullet, the tainted density of which constricted my laboured breathing. The temperature dropped instantly as my skin prickled to the glare of menacing white orbs, watching me intently through the darkness.

Death watched me through the darkness.

An oppressive feeling of choking fear overwhelmed me as the walls seemed to stretch and contract at obscure angles as though a vast throat was sucking the air out of my lungs. As I desperately tried to catch my breath, I realised that no matter how hard I inhaled, I couldn't get enough oxygen in. I convulsed helplessly against the paralysis, but this only induced more panic.

I weakly sucked in the decaying taste of an unknown substance—a potent flavour of something unclean. Somehow, I was falling through space but on my bed simultaneously. No glimmer of light intruded my surroundings, but the shadows of my room still danced and wriggled, overlapping each other, until they began to resemble a more human-looking form.

Although I couldn't see them, I imagined this manifestation's unseen eyes stretched wide, daring me to meet them with my own. Any sense of normality appeared to have been starved from the atmosphere. Digested by the bowels of whatever lurked close by.

Resigned to the overwhelming notion that death now joined me, I prayed for sleep to come and transport me to the morning. But that thought offered me no mercy. Familiar sounds, which generally gave me no cause for concern, at that moment screamed through my organs, electrified with malicious intent. The murmur of cars rattling through the streets, the thump of a door closing, the distant voices of those walking home under the blanket of dusk. Each echo lit up my senses like electrified pins prickling my skin. I knew the threatening presence to be glaring at me, charged with absolute malice, as it commanded my attention.

Paralysed with abject terror, I heard the floorboards settling under the weight of whatever it was that stood near me. Not for a second did I doubt that this demon was there to harm me, its soul tuning into mine, malevolent and consuming. I trembled uncontrollably at the thought of what unclean horror lurked before me.

I remained there until dawn, under the watchful eye of my unwelcome companion, who compelled me to observe its glare, unrelenting within the darkness. However, the insidious nature of its visit seemed betrayed by the dying night, and as time wore on, its grasp diminished further. It wasn't until the light penetrated the windows in the morning that it finally escaped my awareness.

The following evening was much worse. My mum and dad were out at the local pub; therefore, I set myself up on the sofa to wait for them, away from the inconspicuous aperture of my uninvited guest. I was reading some comics to try altering the polluted climate that had lingered since the night before. Still, whenever my eyes gave up and glazed over, I felt a cold and distant gaze fix upon me. The same look Charlie had given me as he disappeared amongst the reeds.

Had he died? Or did we leave him there alive?

I briefly considered wandering back to the park to survey the area. Or would it be better to have called the police? Tears began to fill my eyes as I pondered my predicament. Every inch of my being began to scream out for me to check on Charlie, to tell someone where he was, but at the same time, an overwhelming chill ran through me like electrified ice. An unseen certainty that it didn't matter what course of action I was to take, that something unstoppable was coming for me. And if we led someone to find the dead body of Charlie, it would be Jack and I that would face the blame. At that moment, a vision entered my mind of the police leading me away from my parents to meet my punishment.

Making peace with the concept of riding this out, I tried to blunt the intrusion upon my thoughts and concentrated on my comic. Focussing on each word initially helped, but it caused my heavy eyelids to hold every blink a little longer until, eventually, tiredness led me back into the dark.

I was shocked back into reality with a painful jolt of lightning coursing through my body. The sound of violent footsteps pounded down the hallway, and I cowered as the door flew aggressively open. The weight of a heavy substance stopped hard against the sofa, and I nervously glanced up to see the silhouette of something towering above me. A grey shape which caused a judder of hysteria to shake my foundations. Its obscure face was utterly devoid of all character. It had no eyes, mouth, or nose, but something wriggled beneath its canvas of blank white skin.

I screamed in a voice that couldn't have been mine and awakened alone in the darkness.

The recent nightmare dispersed to the noise of frantic knocking on heavy wood. The vibrations shook through my flesh and were followed by a morbid and occupied silence. It sounded like the clamour had come from my front door, but who would knock with such ferocity? The quiet was equally unpleasant. It was as if the building was holding its breath, fearful of disturbing that which approached.

I checked my watch, and it was half past midnight.

Perhaps I was still dreaming, or my dad had forgotten his keys.

But then, the pounding returned, its new urgency joined with a thick density of menace which swirled around me in the polluted air.

An inhuman knocking.

Slumping quietly off the sofa, I froze immediately as the onslaught escalated, its intensity clawing away at my sanity. Unrecognisable words bellowed from nearby as I carefully moved into the hallway. The unexpected cold within the darkened corridor surprised me, and I gasped audibly at its icy thickness. The grey smoke of my breath clouded in the dark, and I huddled my arms into my chest. Goosebumps on my skin became countless hands reaching for me out of walls that boomed and rattled in synch with the rhythmic banging.

It seemed to take an unnatural amount of time to get to the kitchen. As I pushed the door open, the moonlight bled in as a blue glow, illuminating the tiled floor. Creeping onto my hands and knees, I took a few measured seconds, then peered out of the porthole above the sink that overlooked the balcony. It unsettled me how much gloom it was soaked in. It was as if even the moon's light was reluctant to reveal whatever was buried in the shadows.

A movement caused me to lurch back down below the sink. In response, the thing outside proceeded with its pounding tirade. As I waited in horror, I noticed familiar voices breaking the reticence downstairs. Gingerly peeking out the kitchen window, I saw my mum and dad staggering into the tenement entrance. A mixture of excitement and panic constricted my breathing as I realised they would soon meet this impatient visitor on the stairwell.

I froze deathly still on the kitchen floor until I heard their footsteps clattering on the landing, followed by the jingle of keys in the lock. As I listened to unbalanced footfalls coming from the hallway, I half expected Old Charlie to burst into the kitchen, racing toward me with his arms outstretched.

The light blinked on, and my mother filled the doorway, looking at me with annoyance and drunken confusion.

"What the fuck are *you* doing there? Get yourself to bed!"

I retired to my room but remained wide awake until the morning arrived.

The next evening, my mum sent me to bed early, telling me that I looked like a zombie and needed the rest for my first day at 'grown-up' school. She hadn't mentioned finding me petrified the night before in the kitchen and was probably too drunk even to remember our brief interaction. Or had I been dreaming? At this stage, I was too tired to give anything much thought. I considered again sharing my burden, but this notion was immediately disarmed by the certainty of the authorities removing me from my parents. Maybe leaving a man to die was just as bad as murder?

They argued again as I lay in bed, and my anxiety amplified in response. My resolve toyed with the idea of attempting my meditative state, but my subconscious afforded that to be a terrible idea. One that would likely make me more vulnerable to whatever was trying to reach me. The argument finally ceased with the sound of a slammed door, and all that stirred within the night was the bellows of the ice cream van. Eventually, the darkness swallowed the final remnants of noise and light, feeding them to the creatures roaming the night.

I remained under the glare of my bedside lamp, desperate to stay awake, but the night had other ideas for me. A stirring in the dark corner of my room, untouched by the lamp, began to arrest my curiosity. Although I was awake and in control of my faculties at this point, it didn't seem to matter to whatever approached gently from nearby. A scream stuck in my throat as its unseen form shuffled across the carpet whilst a high-pitched piercing noise reverberated everywhere around me. This strange sensation was comparable to a distant dentist's drill witnessed from the temporary safety of the reception. I rubbed my ears, but the din continued. The change in pitch matched now with the certainty of something trying hard…to communicate with me.

My eyelids threatened to blink, and I used all my resolve to stop them. But it only took a momentary lapse for them to shut, just for a second, for the paralysis to subdue me. I knew immediately that whatever approached me was the same thing pressing against my ribcage with such severity that I struggled to breathe.

Even though I could not see them, I knew the walls to be somehow contracting and twisting obscurely. An immediate sense of imminent dread followed, and I tried to scream for help, but my efforts were rendered useless and silent by the same force which held me to my bed. My gaze was drawn to an abnormally tall figure just outwith my line of vision. So tall it was that it had to stoop to fit its terrible structure under the ceiling. I also knew it to be staring at me, willing me to look around and meet its snarling venomous glare. The floorboards groaned under its heavy tread as it moved closer, taking no pains to move softly as it neared.

A level of inconceivable fear began to overwhelm me. As did a wriggling certainty that my life would be ripped away in an instant if I managed to see this abomination. Its gaze challenged me to turn my head around and set eyes upon it, but I fought with every inch of my fibre not to look. The floorboards creaked again under the weight of its awkwardly creeping form. Part of me began to disconnect from the horror unfolding before me, and it was as though my soul was being channelled away from my body. I also recall a faint chanting. No... not chanting... it was more like mystifying words desperately screaming at me from within. The high-pitched tone was everywhere at this point, rising to a torturous crescendo for what seemed like an eternity.

Unexpectedly and without warning, the form of the presence flooded away into a pool of blackened dust, and everything slowly returned to normal again. As I waited, poised in anticipation for my visitor to return, I heard the morning birds singing to indicate the arrival of dawn. Warm light penetrated the residual darkness, which reluctantly released me of its paralysing grasp. As the certainty of the new day filled my lungs with its nourishment, the remnants of my visitor remained in the atmosphere as a stark warning of the fragility of my existence.

Death is but a catalyst.

My mother and father were waiting for me in the kitchen. It was odd how civil they acted after yet another heated argument. A fried Scottish breakfast was ready for me on the table for my first day at *'big boy school.'* My juvenile mind worked tirelessly to convert the events over the weekend into nothing more than a nightmare. Anything was better than the alternative. I managed to convince myself that as long as I attained an appropriate amount of distance, just like I did with loud noises, I had a chance to escape these hallucinations. Agreeing that my imagination was to blame, I sat down to treat my rumbling stomach to mouthfuls of square sausage, tattie scone and crispy bacon. The TV was on in the background, and the image on the screen caused me to drop my fork noisily onto the plate. Noticing my sudden look of horror, my dad followed my gaze to the TV, which displayed a single headline. The words displayed under a live view of the bridge across from the estate pounced out at me, and in reaction, my heart boomed loudly in my throat—the same rhythm as the front door thumping from two nights previous.

UNIDENTIFIED BODY FOUND IN ROSSHALL PARK.

CHAPTER 2

2004

"It's been a long time, my friend."

His voice was raspy, and his face a deep shade of red. His aftershave was ineffective at masking the sickly smell of dampness from his clothes. Nevertheless, I still recognised Jack, who stood up to welcome me, and I allowed him to pull me tightly into a bear hug.

Jack hadn't aged very well at all. In fact, for someone in his mid-twenties, Jack looked at least twenty years older than the rest of us. His once thick brown mane was thin and wiry, even grey in areas. His eyes were like dark voids, and his unkempt jumper and loose-fitting jeans did little to hide his now scrawny appearance. Jack also projected an underlying demeanour which betrayed that something deeper was morbidly different about my old pal. His disposition hinted at the burden of an untold secret weighing heavily on his narrow shoulders.

"Jesus, Jack," I stuttered, "when did you get home?"

"This morning, mate, I found out you guys would be here, so I thought I might join you."

It is fair to say that Jack had gone off the rails as a teenager, which was one of the reasons we eventually drifted apart. His mother kept some questionable acquaintances, and Jack became drawn into this unhealthy circle. Consequently, the older we got, the guys and I spent more time away from him. I was sixteen the last time I saw him.

I always felt guilty that I should have supported Jack when things started going wrong for him. However, time seemed to have moved on with such haste back then. And as selfish as it was, our secret was always easier to forget without him there.

Jack stepped back to look at me and slapped my shoulder several times with his hand.

"Been working out, man? I have to say; you are looking pretty good, mate. White shirt, blue jeans, textbook stuff. It looks as if time has been kind to you, huh?"

I discerned a slight suggestion of jealousy tainting his words. As a late developer, I eventually matured well into my frame. But even though Jack was much less of an alpha male presence than before, he still projected an air of authority, making me feel small.

For a few hours in that bar, we were children again. We reminisced about all the assholes we had encountered back in the day and our useless attempts at chasing the girls. Jack reminded us of all the times he had protected us, and we laughed helplessly at all the countless stupid things we had done. From sneaking out late to go ghost hunting, walking for miles to the swimming baths and back to save bus fare money to spend on sweets instead, to staying up all night watching movies or playing video games.

Jack reinvigorated the stories we shared and brought them to life, his presence the missing jigsaw piece from growing up. I was transported back to when I observed the world through a different, more innocent lens.

During those rare gatherings, I could usually step out from underneath my habitual shadow momentarily. Although I carried a sense of envy for their ignorance of my sheltered existence, it would generally wash away as each of them in turn took the lead to share stories of their loved ones and ambitions for the future. Concepts I would likely never understand, but I would nod along nonetheless. Their shared experiences were my only link with normality. My light in a world of shadows. But Jack's unexpected attendance reflected my inherent façade, and my walls of protection began to crumble away.

As Jack listened to the guys talking about adult lives far removed from childhood, I spotted another flicker of jealousy in his expression. He seemed to be listening to them intently but was also somewhat detached from the situation. Jack began to wrestle with his every response, and with each sip of his drink, he muttered only a slight acknowledgement to whoever was speaking. No one else noticed Jack's distant demeanour until it was his turn to share his whereabouts for the past few years. In response to this enquiry, he shook his head and said, "Nowhere good", then headed off to replace the drinks. Before we had a chance to delve, Todd put his hands up to signal us all to just leave it for now.

On his return, Jack took the opportunity, as Josh, Shaun, and Todd were amidst a heated debate about football, to lean in and ask me a question that caught me somewhat off guard.

"Had any nightmares recently, mate?"

I could feel my forehead crease into a frown as I met his bleary-eyed gaze.

"Nope, not recently. I think I may have grown out of all that stuff now…finally."

I forced a laugh in an attempt to subdue that particular conversation before it had a chance to develop any further.

"You think that all that stuff was in your head? Even after *all* this time?" Jack scoffed and sipped his beer.

"Absolutely. We nearly scared ourselves to death over all that stuff, but that is all behind us now."

"So, you haven't had any *visits* lately, then?"

I detected something morbidly unsettling about Jack's tone. His demeanour was tainted with annoyance at my apparent indifference to his inquiry. It took me a long time to control my sleep paralysis and develop an ability to predict when an episode was about to occur. Additionally, I learned to take the same measures to prevent any night terrors from manifesting in my imagination. For reasons unknown at the time, though, with Jack present, my mind soon drifted back to that evening by the river. I bit down on my tongue and could taste the metallic hint of blood as I forced those memories back into the unconscious prison I had designed for them. I swallowed hard as thoughts of Old Charlie disappearing into the weeds flashed in my mind more intensely than they had in a while.

Shaun's theatrically excited voice interrupted my attention.

"*Shots.*"

Shaun danced gleefully with his arms as he shuffled towards

the bar to order our drinks.

Jack grinned pensively, and I could see the gears turning in his eyes.

"You and I *really* need to talk, mate."

1991

Jack returned to Glasgow with his mum and stepdad, rejoining us in secondary school. It had been over two years since anyone had seen or heard from him, but as it usually was with good buddies, it quickly seemed like we had never been apart.

Like many others of our age in that particular school, my friends and I struggled. Sure, learning was challenging when you had thirty pupils and one teacher, but we also had to deal with some of the worst future criminals who frequented several classes ahead of us. Some of these 'characters' are likely dead or serving time in jail now, and one of them was a boy called Jason Thomas.

To sum him up, Jason Thomas was quite plainly a vile-natured sociopath, but you wouldn't have gathered that from his appearance alone. With long blonde wavy hair which flowed over his broad shoulders, he could have looked almost feminine had he not been so rough around the edges. His dimpled grin would stretch across his face to greet you, and you never knew if his smile was sincere or if he was thinking about engaging in whatever nasty surprise he had in store. Jason always wore the same blue Adidas tracksuit, and each finger on his right hand had a gold ring jammed below the knuckles.

Sleep paralysis afflicted me on numerous occasions since what had happened with Old Charlie, but it was Jason Thomas who had gifted me the most restless nights. For reasons only known to him, Jason developed a severe and unnatural dislike for me as soon as he saw me. It commenced with the odd remark about my acne and rapidly developed into regular threats and intimidation each time I was unlucky enough to cross his path. On one occasion, he beat me so severely that I wet my trousers in front of my classmates. Rendered helpless by Jason's formidable stature, they followed the path of least resistance by pointing and laughing at me as I ran to the toilet to clean myself up. My mum noticed how withdrawn I had become. Although she expressed a great deal of concern, keeping things from her was probably best. Who knows what other secrets would bleed out along with my tears? Besides, she had her own problems to deal with. We all do.

When Jack returned, however, Jason began to back off slightly; he was genuinely intimidated by him. With Jack by my side, I regained a degree of confidence which allowed me to achieve a sense of normality. I felt completely safe in his company. He and I used to fantasise about getting revenge on Jason for his bullying. If only we had, maybe my dog would still be alive.

Worried as they were about the amount of crime in the area, my dad bought a German Sheppard called Max. Max was a fantastic family dog. Loyal and attentive, as most dogs are, he was content in his own little dog world. He didn't need much to be happy. Just love and warmth, and in return, his affections were unmatched by any human. Max loved being outdoors, and in the summer, my friends and I would take him to the park. We would spend hours there, taking turns throwing the ball for him whilst he raced around in circles. When I was old enough, I was allowed to take him out alone at night, which was quite handy for walking my friends home. If I were at one of their houses, my mum would meet me later with Max, and the three of us would go home together.

One evening, as I was escorting Jack home, Jason Thomas crossed paths with us. Although his devilish stare fixed on me as he approached, I knew he would never dare start anything with me whilst Jack was there, not to mention my dog. Max picked up on his threatening demeanour, and I remember the lead stretching as he lunged at Jason, who, in reflex, leapt back and twisted his ankle on the kerb. A furious sneer filled his face as he snarled at us, "You guys are dead!"

With Jason hobbling away and muttering under his breath, Jack and I shared a laugh before continuing our journey onwards. Graffiti marked several buildings on Jack's street, and many windows were boarded up. Although it was quiet in the early evening, there was still a very unsettling atmosphere about the place, and the threat of violence and crime hung in the air like a bad smell. Before I left him, Jack asked me if I was ok getting home and if he should call my dad because Jason was on the prowl. I dismissed this jokingly, stating something about the dog biting Jason's balls the next time he saw him. After leaving Jack, I chose a different route home to avoid bumping into Jason again.

My detour turned out to be a grave mistake. Jason must have followed me. He ambushed me as I walked down a narrow lane between a forest and the play park.

I heard the sickening crack of a rock crashing into Max's skull, and he immediately dropped to the floor beside my legs. Laughter bellowed beside me as Jason stepped out from behind a tree.

"Serves that fucking mutt right!"

Jason smiled from ear to ear as he advanced, but as he got closer, he realised that the dog was seriously injured. The apparent severity of his actions caused the colour to drain out of his face, followed by the disappearance of his nasty smile.

Max whimpered once last time as his paws slowly curled up into his body. Jason glared at the dog. It was the first time I had ever witnessed fear in him. He then produced a knife from his leather jacket and pointed the blade at me.

"Fuck off", he whispered callously. "And if you tell anyone what I did, I will use this knife to stab your entire family."

Tears bled from my eyes as I crouched to place my hands on my beloved dog.

"I said, *fuck off!*"

"But what about my dog?"

"I don't give a shit. Tell your parents he ran off for all I care. But if I hear any police sirens tonight, I will be straight around your house with all my pals to teach you a lesson. And I know some very nasty people."

Upon arriving home, I told my dad that Max had run away, but he surmised from my appearance that I wasn't being truthful. When he enquired further, I immediately burst into tears and told him everything. My mum called the police, and my dad went to the woods to look for Jason and our dog. But neither the police nor my dad had any luck. Jason had vanished along with Max.

This was the talk of the school over the next few months, and no one seemed to know where Jason was. The police questioned his sidekicks, but no one admitted to seeing him. One or two even approached me to express their condolences for what Jason had done and that they would deal with him unless the police got to him first.

It was several months later that I crossed paths with Jason again. I was cycling back from my part-time job pushing trolleys for the local supermarket when he stepped out in front of me from behind a bus stop. At first, I didn't recognise him. A dark hood was pulled over his head, and he had a scarf over his mouth and nose. But as his eyes lit up with a flicker of excitement, I knew precisely who it was standing before me. He pulled the scarf down to reveal a cruel sneer and gripped my handlebars with his ring-covered fingers. His other hand brandished a large knife.

"Give me your bike", he snarled at me.

In reaction, I jumped off the saddle and stepped away. However, Jason was clearly disinterested in his bounty. He immediately dropped the bike to the floor before carefully surveying the area around him, obviously checking to see if there were any witnesses.

"Do you *know* how much you have fucked up my life, you *fucking* grass?"

His voice was shrill, and his demeanour carried an insidious level of intent. As he neared me, I shuffled backwards with my arms up, but he lashed at me with the knife. His eyes glazed over as he recklessly slashed the air to try and sear my flesh. Terror rendered me incapable of defending myself effectively, but somehow I managed to get hold of his wrist in the melee. I felt a sudden jolt of excruciating pain as his fist smashed brutally into my jaw. A white flash glazed my vision as I stumbled backwards, my legs collapsing awkwardly underneath me. My head cracked audibly on the floor, and Jason was on top of me straight away, continuously swinging the blade as I helplessly lifted my arms to stop him.

I assumed to have fended him off when his attack slowed to a halt, but as he stood above me, I could make out a sudden change in his disposition. A bystander across the road was shouting at him to leave me alone or something of the sort. Jason looked at me one last time and swung a hefty kick at my face, knocking me out cold.

I woke up afterwards in the hospital. Jason's assault had cost me my front teeth, several scars on my arms and a dislocated jaw.

Once again, Jason went back into hiding, but his absence was short-lived. Not even two weeks passed before he ended up in jail with several other gang members that kicked a young boy to death outside a local youth club.

Although the sleepless nights I suffered from Jason's tirade of bullying had initially diminished with the arrival of Jack, my anxiety levels had remained a constant presence. I did expect things to get better, however, with Jason behind bars, but that turned out not to be the case.

Adolescence had been tough, but I imagine it could have been much worse had Jack not been by my side. It was just unfortunate that after my final interaction with Jason, Jack began to convey an interest in that secret we beheld. Since that night by the river, my thoughts had constantly been threatened by the scattered remnants of Old Charlie's demise. It always felt like something was watching me from the shadows and desperately trying to reach me. The less attention I offered those memories, however, the more resilient my defences became. My mind became conditioned to subconsciously attack these infestations on my resolve.

But Jack's regular expression to discuss what happened

seemed to be his way of dealing with things head-on, which allowed a flood of unease to penetrate my protective walls. By compromise, I only entertained debate on this subject whilst we were at his house, not mine. Selfishly, over time, I understood this not to have any lasting effect on my disposition, and consequently, I remained in control of my night terrors.

During subsequent conversations between us, away from the safety of my own house, I discovered that Jack had received the same treatment as I following our interaction with Charlie – in fact, he had suffered much worse. Jack told me his hair had even fallen out due to those nightmarish visitations. We summarised that the same presence must have attached itself to us since we had been the catalysts for Old Charlie to die alone amongst the reeds.

Jack's experience on the first two visits was almost identical to mine, but my blood ran cold as he told me about the third night. Jack had made eye contact with his unwelcome guest on that final evening, whom he swore to be the apparition of Old Charlie. He had screamed desperately at Jack, bellowing unfathomable utterances at him, as Jack lay pinned to the bed.

A few weeks later, Jack shared a revelation that shocked me to the marrow of my bones. He knew someone that had spoken to the police officers who found Charlie dead by the river. It transpired that Charlie's cause of death was confirmed as heart failure, which we already understood. But the time of death likely occurred only moments before he was detected, meaning he had lain there by that river for no less than three days. If he had only been noticed sooner, it was expected he may have survived.

"Wait for a second, Jack. That was not Charlie's ghost haunting us then."

As the words left my mouth, I reminisced back to those three nights of visits, which up until then, we had understood to have been the spectre of Charlie's anguished soul.

I breathed heavily and shook my head in a concentrated exclamation of relief. At that moment, a wave of relief washed over my skin, but my respite faltered as Jack shared words I wished I could erase from my memory.

"Not exactly. What if the old guy was communicating with us somehow from where he lay? We *were* the last two people that saw him alive."

My blood ran cold as I started to understand his angle.

"What if he was trying to tell us that he was still alive and needed help?"

I had tried to absolve all responsibility that we had left

Charlie there to die, convincing myself that nature had simply taken its course and it had been just an accident. We were not to blame. But what if we had just checked on him before scurrying away or called the police? *Might he have survived?*

This revelation gave Jack something else to get his teeth into. Although I was content to leave it well enough alone, he couldn't ignore that invisible itch. He just had to keep scratching away the protective barrier, looking for some kind of closure.

Over the next few months, Jack persuaded me that we had to test the theory that Charlie had somehow reached out to us for help, not from the grave, as we had initially perceived. At first, I was reluctant to give it any consideration. But after weeks of pestering me, he managed to convince me it was the only way for sure to see things through and finally put the memory to bed. By then, Jack was already well aware of my secret routine to deal with the noise of my parents' arguments. I also explained the trance to him, which helped me unwind and subsequently caused repeated bouts of sleep paralysis. Unknown to me, Jack had copied my routine to shut out the sounds of his mother arguing with her new boyfriend, which worked for him. Of course, since Charlie's visitations, I had ceased this for fear of repeat exposure to anything sleep paralysis related.

Unwilling at first to entertain doing this myself, Jack agreed that I could simply watch whilst he tried achieving the necessary state. We practised for several months. I would coach and observe Jack's attempts at travelling through those mazes of tunnels to try and explore beyond the light in which sleep began. The most that tended to happen was that Jack would simply drop off and fall asleep. It was laughable at best, at least until Jack managed to convince me to give it a try for myself.

Every night for the next few weeks, whilst Jack watched, I would sit on his bed and close my eyes. It quickly became straightforward enough for me to simply drop into the trance and fly away from the chimes of reality into the strange network of tunnels that led underground. It seemed easier to control each time, and I found that the more effort I put in, the swifter my approach was to the light at the end, which I now imagined to be a white glowing orb. Most efforts ended with waking up, but on one occasion, I finally entered the rich beam of luminescence whilst suppressing my body's instinct to react. I was then somehow floating above my body whilst Jack watched the ordeal with an excited grin. We had read books about experiments on *OBE*s and how one doctor had placed a note on the shelf above his subject. Once the subject awoke from the self-inflicted trance, he could relay each word written on that sheet of paper.

Panic stopped my journey when my 'outer consciousness' reached the ceiling, and I never got to see the message Jack had left inscribed on his *Etch a Sketch* on the cupboard above his bed. My eyes opened, and as I frantically told Jack what had happened, he seemed to absorb every word. It was so profoundly terrifying and impossible to quantify that I couldn't begin even to consider what lay beyond that point. A compelling sense of being so close to death was as far along the network as I was willing to travel.

To Jack's dismay, I immediately gave up tampering with such things, and this was the precursor for our friendship to slowly fade away. The common thread that had bound us since childhood had lost its rigour, and we suffered many arguments due to our incompatible grievances. From that moment on, I began to adapt my life to distance myself from my anxieties and the particular trance that led to places I had no intention of visiting. Eventually, I learned to suppress any negative feelings and bury them in the back of my mind—a concept that caused me to become more reclusive. At the time, it was a sacrifice I accepted. For me, anything was better than the alternative.

2004

Jack and I headed to the bar to replenish the shots for the guys. Once there, we decided to have a few quick ones before returning to the table. Throwing back my mouthful of foul-tasting Sambuca, I swallowed reluctantly and exhaled slowly to refrain from vomiting. I hated that stuff! I expected Jack to get back onto the subject, which concerned me was the purpose of his visit. I was tempted to ask him where he had been for the last few years and the reason for his gaunt appearance. Still, he had a knack for burrowing in whenever I opened my mouth.

"Remember when we used to do those rituals, mate, trying to have an *Outer Body Experience*?"

Jack downed his shot, cracked it on the bar, and ordered some replacement drinks as he awaited my response. Brain fog caused me to become light-headed as a memory leaked into my awareness like poison from an injected needle.

It never occurred to me that I would end up once again discussing the subject of an *OBE*—an idea I had finally persuaded myself to be fanciful. Whether I believed that or not, I had made peace with the notion that ignorance is bliss.

"Yeah, back in the day, eh?"

I laughed mockingly and met Jack's gaze, trying to disarm the need for further discussion about this nonsense.

However, Jack was keen to continue.

"When my mum dragged us away again after my… stepdad died, I started researching everything I could find about that stuff."

It was then I noticed Jack gazing over my shoulder. He was staring intently at something as he spoke. A cold tingle crawled over my skin. It was as if each hair on my body was attracted to something which displaced the very air around me. I quickly turned to assess Jack's field of vision, but nothing looked out of the ordinary. The bar was half full of regular people going about their everyday lives, drinking and laughing whilst embracing the atmosphere and alcohol buzz. The clinking of glasses, the murmur of indistinct chatter, the cash till sliding open and closed. Focussing on these noises was always my way of tuning out any emotions of dread or fear. But with Jack present, each sound was stifled by an underlying threat of insidious nature.

As he continued to speak of events I wished to be kept hidden, I reluctantly drifted back to his voice.

"I always remember that when Old Charlie died, it was like a door had opened, one that led to a place we were reluctant to fully explore at the time."

I remembered the countless times we practised these ridiculous rituals together. We were obsessed with it all, but that was years ago. And I had called time on all that nonsense.

"Have you ever heard of astral projection?"

Jack smiled, and as he waited again for my answer, he looked over at the guys who were signalling impatiently with their hands for more drinks.

The bar was starting to fill up, and I was beginning to feel on edge.

Reverberations of the live band in the background doing their equipment checks for the evening's entertainment and the pinging of the fruit machine all contributed to a sense of normality – sanctuary even. Familiar echoes of the ordinary danced around in the pub's ambience, but my grip on reality was tiring. It was as if my senses were tuning in to a frequency conjured by Jack's insistence to discuss the secret we shared.

"*Astral projection?* Never heard of it."

I wanted to halt this conversation in its tracks. I spent much of my younger years thinking aliens and ghosts were visiting me. That was until I realised it was more likely to all be a symptom of sleep paralysis. Science-proven rationale disarmed the need to face anything sinister hiding in the dark. The subject still terrified me and was one of the many things I tried to close away in a box inside my head.

"Whilst an OBE is the ability to project your soul out of your body, astral projection is the ability to go further. It's what Charlie would have had to do to reach us from the river."

Jack spoke of these words from a book as if they were simply indisputable facts, and I began to feel claustrophobic in response to the world tightening around me. The din of the bar appeared to be moving further away as something else threatened my nerve.

"Nice! Hey, let's get these drinks back to the table."

My voice was shaky and betrayed my hidden panic. Picking up the tray of shots for the guys, I attempted to walk away from the confrontation, but Jack stepped in front of me.

"Look over there at how blissfully unaware of all of this our pals are. Don't you miss that?"

A cursory glance over Jack's shoulder showed Josh, Shaun and Todd to be in high spirits as they laughed and joked with each other. Any problems hidden behind their glowing faces would pale compared to the burden Jack and I had carried all that time.

"They have no idea of the things we have seen. Look at them; you can tell they are genuinely happy. Unlike us living a lie."

I tore my gaze away and locked eyes with Jack to try and conceal the deceit.

"I am happy, Jack. The past is in the past. Let's leave it at that."

Before he had a chance to respond, I returned to the table with the drinks. I knew he wouldn't discuss this subject in front of anyone else. The secret had always been ours alone. With my body shaking, I sipped heavily on my drink, hoping the alcohol would wash away the fervour of impending doom that choked the pub's climate. Jack rejoined us and, for a while, said no more on the matter.

For the rest of our time in the bar, we reminisced about our childhood together. Each happy memory complemented every cold beer and the occasional gut-retching shot. Only the memories Jack and I shared were kept off the table for discussion. Occasionally we made eye contact, and a knowing look flickered between us very briefly.

We left the pub for the local sports bar to play pool a few hours later. Thankfully the sour atmosphere adulterating the previous location seemed to have dispersed. We had an ongoing pool championship, which had run for years, and on a catch-up such as this, there was no way we would miss the opportunity to crown the new champ. The regular clank of pool balls pocketed underneath a television on the wall whilst supping a cold beer was my favourite taste of normality. A routine which served to top up my endorphin levels. Next, it was onto *The Bunker*, a pleasant and cosy wine bar we liked to frequent during our catch-ups. I preferred my nights out to be in places I felt safe, as it was easier to keep control of my thoughts.

My sense of tranquillity soon proved to be a short-lived condition.

The initial excitement of winning at pool had lifted my spirits, but this sentiment quickly faded. It was as though my positive energy was draining rapidly through a fracture in my sanity. I remember hoping that the effects of the alcohol, mixed with Jack's appearance, had created this unsettling sensation. Unfortunately, this was not the case, and my mindset fully yielded to the poisonous arrival of something unseen.

My attention was arrested by an intense tingling which vibrated through my innards, accompanied by a potent and foul odour. I understood this initially to be coming from the toilets. Something, I know not what, made me turn around. My friends' voices dulled to silence as I glanced toward the restrooms, and a low, piercing ringing rumbled in my eardrums. Someone was standing between the two doors—abnormally tall, horribly slim, wearing a long black jacket with the hood pulled up over his head. What bothered me most was that this figure stood inhumanly still, invoking a familiar sense of unease in me.

I drew my eyes away for a moment and tried to blink away some of the drunken haze that may have been causing this weird impression. Still, as I returned to look again, it was observing me with absolute intent. A strange sense of déjà vu washed through me, waking up deep horrors long forgotten. I had experienced this almost every time I had one of my sleep paralysis episodes in the past, but this only tended to happen when I was asleep and alone.

A feeling of light-headedness started to infiltrate me, and a sudden buzzing in my ears escalated to a high-pitched drilling sound, rising to an almost unbearable crescendo. The pub's walls appeared to stretch concavely like water disturbed by a thrown pebble…or pine cone.

"Are you ok, mate?"

Josh's voice lured my soul back into the grasp of reality.

I ripped my head toward his obscurely spoken words, and it felt like I had just awakened from a vivid dream. Josh was looking at me through narrowed, concerned eyes. Laughing nervously to avert attention to my demeanour, I looked back at the figure by the toilets. But he was no longer there.

"Yeah, I'm good."

I shakily picked up my beer and sipped slowly, trying to disguise my fear from the guys as best as possible. The cold foamy liquid was a welcome relief. Once more, I reluctantly returned my gaze to my watcher, but he remained absent from my consciousness. Back at the table, Jack watched me with eyes just as frightened as mine.

CHAPTER 3

It was still quite early when I left the pub for home. Usually, I would have stayed out later, but Jack's unexpected appearance had soured any source of normality. I just had to get out of there, to breathe fresh air, to walk home over the bridge and through the trees to my safe place, my sanctuary.

A short vibration in my pocket caused me to gasp as I crossed the bridge. It was a text from Jack saying he would pop in and see me tomorrow, stating, "We do still need to chat."

Jack didn't know where I lived, so I ignored the message and continued my journey home. Reencountering Jack had regenerated an old sense of unease, which I was not overly keen to explore.

The park was a much more unwelcoming place at night. A deep blackness had replaced the sun's watchful eye, allowing any nocturnal observers to hide deeper and out of sight. Only a few dim overhead lights penetrated a fraction of the darkness but struggled to control the seeping void which hung beneath the trees.

My heart raced as I approached the ample and empty open space of the park and headed toward the corridor of high trees that led to the edge of my street. The previous colours of the late afternoon had been completely swallowed whole by the gaping yawn of the evening. The deeper I ventured into the park, it was as if the dark was creeping inside and infesting me somehow.

Every single shadow began to take on a more threatening form than expected. It was as if something profoundly terrifying was seeping out of the blackness and reaching for me with hidden fingers. The silence was so consuming that every animal seemed afraid to make a noise for fret of giving away its location.

My heartbeat boomed in my ears as I thought about that presence staring at me in the pub. I envisaged it lurking behind every tree and watching me from every inch of gloom. My blood changed to ice as I discerned a distant but familiar high-pitched tone. What followed was the notion that whatever was watching me in the bar, whether in my mind or not, was now right behind me, staring at me—daring me to turn around and cast eyes upon it.

As I entered the forest stretch leading to the park's exit, I broke into a jog, but a suppressing density stifled my movement. It was as though I was wearing a thick cloak which increasingly tightened around my body. The sensation weighed on me significantly, causing my breathing to become laboured. I panicked as a sudden spell of nausea filled my head. The sickness worsened as I perceived the form of an unseen worm burrowing its way inside my head. It also felt like a thickness in front of me was trying to cover my eyes. I managed to focus on the gleam of light, which flickered with the promise of the park's exit. This offered me the strength to keep moving until I finally escaped onto my street. The intensity of my terror gradually faded as I walked across the road and entered the building. Swinging the door shut behind me with a sharp bang, I raced up the stairs and burst through my front door.

Sleep must have come for me around midnight.

I awoke on my sofa and estimated that I must have been out for at least an hour. As my eyes orientated, I noticed that the TV had switched off. The only thing that offered any illumination was the little glance of moonlight shining through the front window.

An oppressive level of anxiety abruptly affected me as my eyes were attracted to a slight movement in the corner beside the balcony door. It was almost like looking into a black tunnel while waiting for a crazed maniac to race out, screaming a deathly wail.

Within that moment, I knew to be helplessly falling into a state recognisable to anyone who has endured sleep paralysis. My body was incapacitated, and a high-pitched shrieking tone manifested in my ears, much more intense than it usually did. The more I tried to move, the more this acute agitation burrowed inside me like a parasitic worm, exposing me to whatever it was that now shared the space with me. I read once before that the more you struggle and panic during an episode, the more intense the episode becomes. The trick was to try and relax with steady breathing. However, this potent turmoil was soaked and dripping with such malevolence that there appeared to be no possible escape.

Although I could hardly breathe, I had no problem observing the unnatural movement of a mysterious creature dragging its way awkwardly towards me across the floor. It jerkily moved closer as if desperate to escape hidden restraints. A wet guttural slopping noise filled the room as the moonlight glare revealed a shiny head, part human, part bone and tissue. Putrescent meat hung off its structure and leaked heavily onto the floor. I fought again to move and scream, but fear rooted me to the spot, forbidding me to do little more than witness my visitor's terrible form. Every wall pulled in my direction as if something was trying to delve through from the other side to reach me. But it was the creature's slow advance that commanded my attention.

White hair ripped out of split rotten flesh, and the darkest eyes I have ever seen opened at the top of its oversized head. Eyes stretched impossibly wide, stared into mine. Its abnormally cavernous mouth sneered at me with abhorrent rage. I smelled and tasted its rotten and inhuman hatred as it uttered a gut-retching scream which caused me to hold my breath in fright.

For how long I lay there afterwards, I cannot seem to recall. The immediate silence that followed this attack gradually yielded to the sound of my heartbeat. As I concentrated on my heart's rhythm, I tried to relax and regain some kind of control. A glaze of dampness grew underneath my freezing skin, and as I tried to wriggle and flex, my efforts wafted up a cocktail of sweat and urine. Whether this was a nightmare or worse, I wished for the morning sun to hurry and release me from this prison of shadows.

The spectral infestation eventually released my body from its paralysed state, almost directly in response to the sound of my ringing phone. A cursory glance around the room confirmed I was alone, and I reached towards the flashing glow of my mobile screen.

It was Jack.

He arrived at my house with a crate of beer later that day. I had ignored his attempts to contact me initially but eventually gave in to his persistence. I decided to hear him out, for what harm would that bring? After cracking open two beers and handing me one, he began to speak words which sent a chill back into my bloodstream.

"I never told you what happened with my stepdad."

Jack explained how he had been lying in bed listening to his mother and stepfather arguing. It was clear to him that his mother tried fruitlessly to calm the situation down while his stepdad burned relentlessly with aggression.

"He used to beat her, you know, sometimes pretty bad."

Jack stared at his beer bottle as he allowed the memory to unfold.

"I used to lie in bed at night, thinking of ways to deal with that bastard."

Jack seemed to ponder for a moment as a weird smile filled his face.

"In the end, what I did... it just transpired so naturally. My anger started to ignite something deep inside of me, and I found myself drawn into the same experience we had all those years ago. Remember that sensation we used to have as we tried to leave our bodies? It was like that, only much stronger and more deliberate this time. I wanted to kill him. The intensity of my thoughts somehow gave me the ability to leave my body like you managed to do, and I could never. But I went further and didn't even stop at the ceiling when I left my body."

My skin prickled as I listened to Jack's story. I knew what he was talking about and waited, intrigued, for him to continue.

"Like we used to practice, I entered the white light which beckoned my inner consciousness. Unlike before, I had no apprehension this time of whatever lay beyond. The rage drove me onwards and upwards, unstoppable."

Jack noticed that the more he focused on his stepdad, the more control he retained. Rage driving him on, he moved closer and closer until he was above his victim, close enough to smell his rancid breath.

I looked at Jack for a short while; each word he spoke was potent with absolute sincerity. This couldn't be for real.

I imagined Old Charlie lurking in the back of my mind and shook my head to try and disregard the hallucination. Jack's words then once again interrupted my thoughts:

"I remember his eyes opening. Panicking in case my mother woke up, I managed to pin him down to the bed as if he was nothing. He looked absolutely petrified. His fear inspired me to apply a little more force right down onto his chest, just the right amount to stop him from screaming for help. I stared into his pleading eyes the whole time as I worked. He was unable to move. Just as though he was having sleep paralysis himself. With each breath he exhaled, I exerted more and more pressure, squeezing the life out of him with this *unseen force.*"

Jack used his hands to emphasise the choking of his stepfather's neck.

"I crushed the life out of him. Right beside my mother. It was crazy. She was undisturbed by the whole affair."

Jack glowed with crazed excitement as he smiled confidently across at me.

"I was convinced it was all a dream when I was back in bed.

But I heard my mother's horrifying scream a few hours later."

Jack told me he ran next door, initially thinking his stepdad was hurting his mum again. He opened the door to find his mother in hysterics. She was fine, but her husband lay there contorted on the bed, eyes wide open and his mouth stretched at an odd angle.

"Astral projection."

Jack breathed out heavily and finished his beer

1994

Jack lay in bed, waiting for the alarm clock to go off. Today was his sixteenth birthday, but he knew that no one cared. Of course, his mother didn't care about anyone other than herself and that asshole she married.

Jack hated him. He was sick of the countless nights of listening to his mother begging for mercy as her flesh absorbed his aggressive fists. Jack had faced him once and once only. The knife against his throat and the threat of his mother being 'gutted' had stopped him in his tracks. He accepted no option other than to suffer and wait for this asshole to get bored and move on to the next victim or go back to jail.

Last year, Jack had located his mother's stash. Primarily cocaine, but occasionally heroin was readily available from the kitchen table as his mother lay passed out yet again, leaving her leftovers discarded. It hadn't taken Jack long to realise that he could make some money from these scraps. Soon, he found a couple of regular buyers who would take whatever was available.

"Sixteen years old," Jack pondered. Was this how his life was going to be?

His oldest friends had even lost interest in him recently, but maybe he didn't need them anymore. Trying to flee his negative mindset, he reminisced about some of the fonder memories of adolescence, but it didn't take long before thoughts of Old Charlie interrupted his recollection.

The three nights of visitations following that fateful interaction in the park had haunted him. Remnants of which remained with him ever since. Old Charlie hadn't visited him for a while, but he knew he would be there when shit got too stressful. Another notion bothered him. He wondered just how long it would be before Charlie exacted his vengeance.

Jack's alarm clock began to chime, and he got up quickly to switch it off and reach for his tablets. He looked at the label of his antidepressants and wondered if he should just throw the lot away. This notion departed him very swiftly. From somewhere unseen, Charlie's gaze fixed upon him, daring him to skip his medication. The pills were the only thing that seemed to keep away the night terrors, including Charlie, for now, at least. But it didn't take much for the doorway to swing open, allowing the frantic manifestations to spill through from hidden worlds to torment his paralysed body. Sometimes he heard the unseen abnormalities speak; on other occasions, the shadow figure Jack knew to be Charlie just stood in silence, watching him from the corner of the room.

Jack shuddered, popped a couple of his capsules, and got ready for his first day as an adult.

That evening, Jack went on to murder his stepfather.

2004

"The nightmares stopped once I dealt with that asshole," Jack casually informed me as we cracked open some more beers.

"Since those visitations we both experienced after Charlie died, I always felt that something was following me. Hiding in the background, dormant, waiting for the right moment and then 'pow,' just like that. Gone."

I exhaled heavily and took another sip of my beer whilst Jack silently pondered his next words.

"We eventually landed on the concept that Charlie was trying to reach us while he was still alive...but I know different now."

Knowing that he had me hooked, Jack now waited for my response. He had dangled the string, and I had taken on the role of the cat.

"Ok, you have my attention. What do you think it was then? More to the point, why do I need to know all of this?"

"I have conducted quite a bit of research into sleep paralysis, my friend," Jack said with a confident tone.

"I now understand that during sleep paralysis, the shadow figure or visitor manifests as a subconscious product of our worries and guilt. Therefore, it makes sense that when we did what we did to Old Charlie, we had this projection of our guilt visiting us, not the man himself."

I pondered back to the day I saw those words on the television screen, words now etched into my mind like an unhealed scar.

UNIDENTIFIED BODY FOUND IN ROSSHALL PARK.

That night, the intense nature of those particular visitations had thankfully ended. Albeit, things didn't *exactly* just end; I just got better at suppressing my emotions and guilt from that moment on. Consequently, the connection to those terrors reduced significantly and continued to dull each night until I completely controlled my symptoms. Although more distant and unable to reach me, Charlie, or whatever my visitor was, was always there, lurking in the back of my mind, always out of sight and slipping further away as my resilience improved.

"And not just that," Jack continued.

"I used to hear that asshole beating my mum. I was crazy with rage but too frightened to intervene, just in case I made things worse. As I listened, the apparition would always return to me to match the intensity of my anxiety. I believe that it materialised as my projected guilt for not protecting her. Or my frustrations for what he was putting her through."

I considered Jack's words. Also understanding a great deal about sleep paralysis, I knew enough to appreciate that the visitor was usually an illusion of your anxiety or even a memory that haunts you. If this much was true, then maybe it was never Old Charlie or even some other malevolent spirit in front of me; it was simply a manifestation of my guilt. It had all appeared so vivid at the time, however.

"And amazingly, no more night terrors since I dealt with my stepdad. No more guilt."

Jack stretched his arms behind his head, satisfied with the expected impact of his story on my disposition. He sat there pleased with himself for a moment, like a magician who had just revealed his secret before reaching into his pocket and producing a folded-up note. After placing it into my open hand, he ambled to the window and stared intently across the park.

I unfolded the piece of paper; it was an address for Jason Thomas.

CHAPTER 4

Only those who have suffered bullying will understand that feeling of worthlessness when someone exhibits control over you, using you for the gratification of their selfish indulgences.

Jason Thomas had not just killed my dog; he also had almost killed me. He was, quite simply put, evil, with absolutely no remorse. Worthless.

I will never forget how many sleepless nights I spent praying for his demise. When he was arrested, he should have gone away forever. Unfortunately, his sentence lasted only seven years. Somehow he had managed to satisfy the quite frankly pitiful justice system and was released well before the end of his term. Jason had scarred me not just physically but psychologically, and I was always secretly desperate to one day exact at least some kind of retribution on him. At the mere mention of his name, my blood chilled as something inside my consciousness was disrupted—a stand of unseen matter still woven into his foul existence. It only took a momentary lapse for my mind to instinctively unravel its weave of protection for the particular set of buried memories involving Jason. With the protective barriers down, my rationality would begin its search for a more meaningful connection to explain this discontent.

Although the life I was fortunate enough to live was satisfactory, deep down inside lurked a longing for much more, a notion that bobbed and floated on the surface of my cognition, teasing me with its promise of an upgraded existence. When I was younger, I had ambition, drive, and a sense of adventure; Jack's return had allowed these repressed tendencies to unlock. It was mentally and physically taxing to ignore the demons of my past, and at that moment, I realised just how small my world had become. By looking deeper, it wasn't long before it became apparent. I had become a victim. Bullies like Jason Thomas would always walk free in the wild, oblivious to the bruises and mental scars they inflicted on others. Unless someone intervened, that is.

My life was reasonably decent, but I didn't have much of a purpose. Other than catching up with my old friends once a year, my interactions with anyone else were nonexistent. I allowed myself to attribute this disconnect from society to the trauma Jason Thomas had afflicted me. What happened with Old Charlie was an accident, and I had made peace with that. It was Jason that had inflicted on me the most significant amount of psychological damage.

Jack presented his plan simply enough. The first thing required was to survey Jason's house and get a layout of his surroundings. Next, I was required to partake in some astral projection before finally taking this asshole out of the game for good. All being well, my nightmares and anxiety would break free of any more visitations or hauntings. It all seemed straightforward enough…

"Jack, this is *insane*."

I laughed mockingly at Jack's proposed plan, even though I had begun to hang on to every word he spoke about this. Jack knew this to be within the realms of possibility, having already done it himself. But could revenge finally be sought upon this poor excuse for a human? *OBE*s were real, and I knew how to self-inflict sleep paralysis; hell, it took more effort to prevent the damn thing. The only stumbling block was the little thing called astral projection. Was this even possible?

"The only *insane* thing here is even considering letting that prick get away with what he has done to you and what he is still doing to people."

Jack informed me that my childhood bully was now a drug dealer and lived less than ten miles away. Gaining the address from an old acquaintance, he had even arranged to pick up some drugs at his place later.

"You seem to have all of this worked out, Jack."

I wondered just what was in this for him. Other than some bygone need to still look out for his old pals. I knew what was in it for me, and I trembled with anticipation at the infliction of some well-deserved revenge. But what was he getting from this?

As I wandered into the park with Jack, my senses felt acutely alive and on edge. I became subtly drawn to the more unexciting interactions of people going about their lives in the immediate vicinity, which confirmed the earlier notion that something was indeed missing within me. And this perception was growing more intense by the minute. My attention was arrested by young couples resting contently in the sun, holding hands or laughing at a private conversation. A couple of pensioners shuffled toward the duck pond carrying old loaves of bread before ripping up a few slices and scattering them at the numerous swans. An excited father helped his son balance on his new bike.

All these people were blissfully ignorant of what secrets hid deep inside their flesh. Each face glowing under the sun, dreadfully unenlightened to that which lay dormant and waiting. Hidden from their unconditioned souls lurks a strand of invisible matter that connects us all. A certainty unnoticed by most until they struggle for their last breath. Guarded within their ignorance, they padded around safely in their regular bubbles, unreached by the unseen creatures concealed within the shadows. And yet each smiling face reflected in my eyes reminded me of everything I was missing out on. A tingling glow in my stomach rose into my heart to whisper the promise that I was on the verge of something sincere.

I decided that Jack's idea may just be precisely what I needed. I couldn't run forever from conflict for fear of opening up repressed memories. Maybe it was time to shake things up and affront the demons of my past.

We had spent the afternoon drinking a bottle of malt I had stored away for a 'special occasion' – I guess this counted. Jack had also guided me through the mechanics of his newfound gift.

According to Jack's experience, sleep paralysis was the doorway to an *OBE*. From that moment, it was about the courage to travel beyond our inferred reality. A strong enough motivation was required to free your spirit into the bright doorway between realms, to bind with this alternate level of being. For me, this portal would hopefully enable me access to Jason Thomas from the shelter of my apartment. It never occurred to me that there might be a cost to exposing your soul to things outside scientific comprehension.

Riding high on the recent whiskey buzz, I watched over everyone in the park as the sun above watched over me. However, this normality didn't last long, and soon I felt other eyes upon me; familiar, long-forgotten eyes, observing my every move.

I tried to ignore my unwelcome observer as we approached the main street and headed for a bench overlooking the pub we had frequented the previous evening. Once seated, I started to focus on any white noise available. Tuning in to the hypnotic chant of traffic murmuring along and birdsong from the trees was enough to prohibit the visitor's presence as we waited for the taxi to arrive.

"So, must we go into this bastard's flat, Jack?"

"I don't, but you do. You need to know how it looks. Trust

me; it's how this will work. You need to know the exact layout, and it needs to be intimate to you. Your physical imprint is key."

The taxi dropped us off deep inside a highly unnerving-looking housing estate. To call it a slum would be too optimistic a description. Three grey blocks of semi-boarded-up flats covered in graffiti commanded our view. Scatterings of dodgy-looking youths gathered in open closes and street corners, smoking joints or drinking cans of beer. The bleak atmosphere of the place was deeply unsettling.

Each building stood twenty floors tall, with open verandas outside each apartment. Every porch was littered with junk and cloaked in wire mesh, no doubt fitted to prevent people from falling over the sides or jumping.

I recalled reading about an asylum-seeking family who had been asked to leave their property at one of those flats by the council. The time to return to their country beckoned, and they had no official grounds to remain. After failing to dispute the right to stay, the father threw his wife and children over the balcony, follwed by himself. Seemingly, some things are worse than death to some.

Abundant waste ground surrounded the tall, foreboding buildings. A centrally located playground was littered with rubbish and graffiti; every item was vandalised to deny any potential for a child's enjoyment. Broken roundabouts, vandalised swings, and a grimy climbing frame were all that appeared to have survived whatever extent of decoration the local youths deemed appropriate. Debris littered the entirety of the surrounding areas. As we approached the centre tower, I became very unnerved at the hiss of paused silence which lingered in the air, and my skin tingled cold, causing me to shiver.

"Are you ok, mate?"

Jack glanced at me, and we paused briefly outside the building.

"Let's just get in and get out. Fast."

Jason Thomas lived on the bottom floor at the centre of the three derelict brick apertures. A place filled with ex-convicts, drug-addled souls and anyone else down on their luck. I didn't quite comprehend how I would feel when I saw him again, but my stomach was already turning with a mix of rage and fear. *Would he recognise me?* With the effects of the whiskey buzz wearing off, I became apprehensive. My fight or flight response threatened to activate at any given time. Blood pumped through my veins at an uncomfortable rate, and I felt mentally connected to every inch of my fibre as the recent cold sensation gave way to the heat infusing my warm and poised muscles.

I had considered the possibility of losing control if he did indeed acknowledge me. I have never been a fighter, but this fucker deserved all that was coming. Brushing my impulses aside for the moment, I followed Jack quietly inside the building, all the way to the gateway of that animal's habitation. As if a zoo for wild animals, every door had a cage around it, and the smell of dampness and strong urine made me instantly nauseous. Not the most welcoming place to visit; this place simply said one thing: *Stay Away!* Jack thumped on the door behind the cage, and we heard footsteps advancing on the other side. I swayed from side to side and had to take a few deep breaths to steady my balance.

The girl who opened the door looked manic, clearly a drug addict. I got the impression that she could have been quite attractive had it not been for the cold sores, the drawn-in face, thin hair, and rotten teeth. She wore a loose-fitting dressing gown partially covering a filthy pair of tracksuit trousers.

"What do *you* want?"

"I was given this address to come and see Jason for some eh…here look, I have money."

Jack showed the girl some folded-up notes. After inspecting

them, she opened the door wide enough to let us in. I swallowed hard, and my jaw tightened as we stepped over the threshold.

The fragrance within the flat was much worse than the smell outside, a sickening and sweet, musty aroma of dampness you would associate with a neglected public toilet. Jack nudged me, and I hastily commenced my survey, recalling his earlier protest that I needed to be aware of the surroundings for this to work. A short hallway led to a tiny kitchen on the left, full of dirty dishes, overflowing ashtrays and randomly scattered needles and powders. Across from the kitchen was a bedroom with random stains on the carpet, a bed piled high with dirty clothing, and a towel acting as a curtain to blot out large damp patches on the walls. Further along, a discarded door leaned against the wall by a small bathroom with a broken toilet seat and countless disgusting blemishes glazed over each porcelain utility. The smell made me gag, and I had to cover my mouth and hold my breath as we passed. The girl led us along the remainder of the apartment, ridden with black mould on the ceiling and other discoloured smudges on the walls. Torn carpets showed dilapidated underflooring. Discarded beer bottles and takeaway boxes made up the rest of the interior décor. Something crunched under my feet as we approached the chamber at the end of the flat.

Sweat raced from my armpits, tickling my skin as it flowed down the sides of my body. We were about to enter Jason's lair, and I was in the realm of having a panic attack. I managed to take a few deep breaths and took a pause to steady myself in the stifling atmosphere. It was time to meet my old nemesis, and it was like I was floating toward him. My throat tickled in response to a strong smell of weed which permeated the other repulsive aromas seasoning the dank air.

I recognised the vile form of Jason sitting on an old leather armchair as techno music bounced out of a TV amidst a hypnotic backdrop. He held a can of beer in one grimy hand and a cigarette in the other.

Jason's previously muscular physique had withered into an almost skeletal, emaciated figure. Slips of bare tattooed skin protruded from his oversized t-shirt, showing off some nasty needle marks and weeping sores. His eyes and mouth, which were far too big for his haggard, cadaverous face, implied a note of familiarity with Jack and me. He enquired with a voice that sounded filtered through a broken radio speaker, displaying a mixture of black and yellow teeth as he spoke.

"Do I know you?"

My toes gripped hard into my trainers, and the muscles in

my feet spasmed painfully. The ability to speak left me as those familiar eyes met mine. Eyes which still caused my blood to run cold. To my relief, Jack quickly answered on our behalf.

"I don't think so, mate, unless you have spent much time in London?"

In response to Jack's lie, Jason smacked his lips and narrowed his blackened eyes, which appeared lost in his pickled skin. He looked at us again individually before shaking his head to dismiss any notion that he knew us.

As per his plan, Jack went on to buy a few bags of cocaine, and we began to make a very swift exit from that creature's cave. I observed more disgust and hatred within my soul for that vile human being than ever as I perused around one last time at his repulsive habitat. My mind was now dead set. This guy was a goner.

"See you later," I scoffed under my breath.

CHAPTER 5

Jack headed off to quickly tend to a *'personal matter'* once we returned from the survey of Jason's surroundings.

Upon arriving home, I took a shower to clean my skin from Jason's filthy nest. Once my clothing was in the washing machine, I sat on the porch to watch the sunset over the distant mountains. Immediately in front, the park served as a welcoming green contrast to the grey and tired city beyond. I imagined it as a protective barrier to normality, to a place I ventured into occasionally but never wished to stay too long. Beyond Glasgow's rising and dipping skyline, vast hills rose to sweeping snow-topped peaks. Behind those hills was a place I promised to explore once all this was over. To seek a new life, a new job, and maybe even a family. I could be as normal as Josh, Shaun and Todd. Once I had nothing left to fear, anything was possible.

But was this possible?

My mind was ablaze, and I started to believe this would work. I was no longer afraid of the prospect of facing my demons. It was time to be released front the grips of this burden, which would hopefully demise in the exact moment as Jason Thomas. The memory of Jason's torrential bullying was one thing, but another impression challenged me. It haunted me that maybe if I had stood up to Jason at school, he might not have gone on to kill my beloved dog or kick an innocent young boy to death.

I closed my eyes to the sound of the washing machine spinning and its vibrations tingled under my bare feet on the cold stone balcony floor. Would things *really* change for me with my childhood bully out of the way? I envisaged Old Charlie and that fateful interaction that proceeded all of this. Although we hadn't expected a man to die, we were just kids; it was nothing more than an accident. Tears filled my eyes as I considered what we had done from my perspective of an adult facing the uncomfortable truth of a previous mistake. Having suppressed so much over the years, I finally began absorbing the guilt for my actions. Any apology I attempted to offer to the memory was met with nothing but regret. I even tried to project my shame and sorrow deeper into my consciousness as forgotten thoughts drained from hidden areas within my brain, but no respite followed.

The washing machine drone reduced to nothing more than a constant white noise, which allowed me to continue my attempt at making peace with the secret Jack and I would carry to our grave. We were responsible for what happened to Charlie. It was that simple.

Carrying a burden such as that is enough to cause anyone to hallucinate and see things that weren't there, especially for one prone to sleep paralysis. Whatever the visitor was, I alone carried it within me; it wasn't real, and it certainly wasn't just one single entity. The materialisations wore the face of whatever I feared the most; my imagination just filled in the blanks and gave it an identity, such as Charlie or, more recently, Jason.

Jason had caused me to have countless anxiety attacks during adolescence. Undoubtedly, he had been the catalyst for the sleep paralysis episodes after my mind built its resistance to the memory of Charlie. Ones where the manifestation usually lurked just out of sight, sneering at me with that familiar dominating presence. A product of my subconscious baggage, which I had learned to suppress over the years for fear that any anxiety trigger would cause my walls of protection to come tumbling down. And at that moment, I began to blame everything on Jason. Each occurrence was simply a projection of Jason, of all that pent-up anger, not Charlie. He was gone, and I needed to make peace with that.

I had read books stating that the visitor was often misinterpreted as a spectre or ghoul. But that it was more likely to be something you carried about with you, perhaps some unfinished business? It seemed to have worked for Jack. I was compelled to see if it worked for me.

*

Jack opened the door to his Grandmother's house and quickly made his way to the room he had stayed in for the last few nights. He only needed a few more days, and then he was gone. His Gran sat quietly by the fireplace and didn't even stir to acknowledge his arrival. Just like his mother before her, she didn't give a shit.

The only person in Jack's world who had any significance to him was his girlfriend. The motivation of her genuine love for him offered a beacon of hope to overcome the notion of backing out from doing this to his oldest pal. Things had gone on for too long, and there was only one way out. He had carried this baggage for too long, and it was now clear he carried it alone.

Jack spent the following few hours pondering whilst snorting several lines of the cocaine he had just purchased. It had to be Jason. He was an essential part of all of this, and his past as a bully would soon be met with a well-deserved punishment. The act of revenge on Jason by Jack's oldest friend should be enough to let Old Charlie in. If only he knew then what he now understood. That crossing over into the OBE carried such a risk. If only he had understood that the monsters in your imagination are genuine and that they wriggled and squirmed so close to the surface of reality.

Monsters that are only rarely seen in our worst nightmares. And that exploration within the void between existence and death empowered those anomalies to see you. And not only see you. Those who explore even further expose themselves to something worse. Within that shared darkness lurk those seeking vengeance on anyone who has wronged them. A collaborative network of malevolent creatures that are profoundly desperate to pursue anyone that may dare to break the threshold of their realm.

He drew one last line of cocaine on the table, and instead of ingesting it immediately, he made a promise to himself. That this would be his final exposure to drugs. As his gaze studied the white powder before him, he let his mind wander back to the bitter memory of when his life had finally spiralled out of control.

On his sixteenth birthday, Jack fought with a guy at school who had spit on him before calling his mum a 'junkie slut'. He had to be dragged off by the teachers and was consequently sent home on suspension. If the teachers hadn't intervened, Jack knew he would have likely beaten him to a pulp. All the rage in his spirit had come alive at that moment, and he had imagined his stepfather to be underneath his vicious onslaught.

On that evening, Jack finally dealt with his stepfather. Something which seemed to happen very naturally. He linked the motivation for his actions with the fact that the recent alteration at school had stirred up his repressed anger, allowing him access to a previously unexplored compulsion. But as soon as his stepfather's groans had lessened to the sweet mercy of death, Old Charlie was there, burrowing nearer to him with every consecutive visit. Each occurrence was palpably more intense and pronounced than the last. Drugs and medication had somehow managed to suppress the means for his visitor to reach him, but they couldn't stop Charlie from lurking in the shadows. And now, Charlie had been granted his beacon of opportunity to share the darkness with Jack every time he closed his eyes. It took him a while to work it out, but Jack soon understood that astral projection had been the precursor to unleashing the monsters from Charlie's domain.

With the drugs now potently stirring within his blood, he began to write a letter. A letter he would pass on to his friend when he next saw him. Providing everything went to plan, that was. And not for a moment did his conscience offer any resistance.

It was time to share this burden. No, it was time to pass on this burden, and the only way to do it had been made clear by Old Charlie on his final visit before stepping back into the shadows to wait...and watch. Even now, he felt Charlie's gaze upon him. Eyes which commanded him to carry out his nefarious task. He paused one last time to contemplate Charlie's final visit.

Jack had awakened in that terrifyingly familiar state of paralysis, his efforts rendered useless by the onslaught of Charlie's advance. The pounding of his heartbeat was loud in his ears as he saw the flicker of movement from the corner of his eye. The figure stood tall under a cloak of blackness that filled the room in abundance. The deep guttural voice that vomited from its hideous mouth froze Jack entirely, his fear thrashing back at him like waves rolling over an empty beach. The extreme sensitivity of absolute terror that followed each visitation was always overwhelming. He tried to shake, move, and scream simultaneously, but the night refused to yield to his efforts.

Jack did not initially understand the sounds which spat from *this evil spectre, but his mind began to translate an increasing urgency to their intent. With slow and purpose-driven steps, Charlie advanced toward him with a demeanour more menacing than anything Jack had ever imagined.*

Panic caused Jack to attempt one last effort to shake free, but his endeavours remained worthless. The intensity of the experience continued to amplify. Charlie's presence had somehow devoured any sense of normality as he neared Jack's paralysed body. Charlie was soon at the foot of Jack's bed, wet and shiny in the gloom. Tufts of white hair were occasionally visible in front of hideous veiny eyes nestling at the top of a melted and torn face.

His jaws finally stretched wide as every hair on Jack's skin reached out in a futile attempt to hold onto the grasp of reality. A mouth abnormally large twisted to showcase a void of darkness even more profound than the one consuming the bedroom. From the gurgled and splattered bellowings it uttered, louder than the sounds of Jack's beating heart, he began to understand the message it carried from the grave.

"*Where is the other one?*"

*

Jack returned at around nine o'clock and encouraged me immediately to try and self-induce sleep paralysis. He seemed very eager to move things along, which at the time didn't play on my mind too much. It had been a while since I had last managed to do it, but at that moment, I wanted it more than anything.

But nothing worked.

Even when I followed step by step the journey which used to lead me there as a child, nothing happened. Jack monitored my attempts to induce the appropriate state of being, but it all felt unnatural, almost laughable. Something was missing. Maybe I had hidden it away too well.

Frustrated at my fruitless efforts, I gave it another attempt. Closing my eyes, I breathed out deeply and focused again on all the nasty things Jason had put me through in my life. It wasn't enough, so I tried to manifest the feelings that used to haunt me. Although tricky at first, I eventually connected with the vivid touch of his fist on my face. The cold steel of his blade lashing out at me. Next, the sickening crack of my dog's skull under the weight of a rock. Even the sensation of my damp trousers from the time he caused me to urinate in front of the class. I felt light-headed, but for whatever reason, I couldn't tune into the correct frequency to travel beyond the dark behind my eyelids. It was as if an ingrained reluctance stopped me from going all the way. After that attempt, I gave up and, much to Jack's frustration, insisted on taking a break.

"You need to take this seriously, mate, or it will never happen."

Jack spoke clearly and directly, like a drill instructor ordering his troops. I also detected a level of annoyance harvesting beneath the surface of his demeanour.

I nodded in agreement whilst avoiding his eyes to conceal any projected negativity. Maybe it had previously worked because my anxieties were more subconscious. Perhaps trying too hard blocked the innate reflex in my body to react to any threat. By making it more of a conscious thing, my brain would recognise this, subsequently rendering sleep paralysis impossible. Resigned to failure, I finally decided to ask Jack a question to which I had given due consideration.

"Jack, what's in this for you?"

Jack placed his empty beer bottle on the table and took another from the box on the floor. He moved with a sense of calm and serenity, opening another beer before he gave an overly measured response.

"What do you mean?"

"I mean. All *this*? It's great to see you and all," I glanced away during the deceit, "but I haven't seen you for years."

Jack nodded as I spoke, his eye contact becoming more intense as the words clumsily spilt from my alcohol-relaxed mouth. He didn't respond; he just waited for me to fill the fragile silence instead.

"You were hanging out with a bunch of *assholes*. You weren't bothered with us when you left."

A flicker of rage glazed over Jack's eyes, only for a second, but I noticed it. His demeanour became more fragile as he appeared to wipe an invisible tear from his eye.

"I always loved you guys. But you and I were like brothers…I needed *you* back then. My mum was taking drugs and hanging about with the wrong crowd…"

"You never said, Jack..."

"I shouldn't have had to. We were best friends. That's just what you do for each other. You should know if your brother needs help."

Stillness lingered between us for a few minutes. In the distance outside, a police car siren wailed towards town. From nearby, a slight wind picked up and caused the blinds to ruffle.

"Jack. I am sorry. But I honestly didn't know how bad things were at home. If I had any idea, I would have helped. We just thought you were bored of us when you started to jump around with those older guys."

Jack stood up and walked to the window. I watched him gazing out over the park and was astonished at how slender he had become. He spoke without turning his head.

"One thing about me. I am loyal to the very end, especially to family..." Jack paused as if distracted by his words, "it's me that should be sorry. Maybe I should have reached out to you guys sooner. But I got swept into a dark place. One I believed I would never get out of..."

He allowed his voice to trail off, then turned to face me again.

"So think of this as my last gift to you. Some unfinished business."

Jack smirked coldly as he spoke. The tone of his articulation unnerved me. His demeanour suggested illness, but I settled against mentioning this, not to draw too much attention to his appearance. He approached me and sat on the sofa, placing a scrawny arm just behind my neck.

"For you, this is a way out. For me, it's just about doing the right thing for someone I love. That's it."

Something inside me didn't entirely accept this as a credible reason, but then again, Jack always did look out for me. His intent was believable, but the measured emphasis of his response seemed to betray an insincerity. As though he wasn't being entirely honest about his rationale. It didn't matter anyway, as I had already made my mind up. Whatever Jack's intent for sharing this gift with me was, I wanted to keep trying. If it failed, what the heck? But if there was even a slight chance it may work, it would be worth it, even if only to unleash my revenge on Jason Thomas.

It must have been around midnight that Jack reached into his pocket to retrieve a clear bag full of pills. He emptied two out and placed them into my open hand.

"Ok, so what are *these* then, Jack?"

I scrutinised the blue tablets, curious as to the purpose they may serve.

"These are called SSRIs. Antidepressants. One of the lesser-known side effects not often highlighted is that they can induce sleep paralysis."

"How did you *attain* these?" I reluctantly enquired. Jack wasn't just a sleep guru; he was also apparently a *medical doctor*.

"I took them a few years ago, after that *business* with my stepdad, and without even trying, I slipped into sleep paralysis, just, like, that," Jack snapped his fingers on the 'that'.

"It's a side effect of the medication and worked fine for me, albeit by accident."

As I scrutinised the powder blue cylinder shapes, which were about the same size as regular paracetamol, I allowed myself to humour the idea for a moment. It may have taken years to recover my suppressed ability to self-inflict sleep paralysis. After a short moment of consideration, I returned the tablets to Jack, who reluctantly replaced them into the clear bag, and again, I noted a significant change in his mood. His shoulders dropped as if he was wrestling against a bitter contempt for my reluctance.

"Why don't you just do it for me, mate?" I wryly enquired. Jack just gazed at me ominously and insisted I must be the one to exorcise my demon. He exhaled heavily and shook his head before leaving me to go and fill up the coffee machine, muttering something under his breath about how caffeine has been identified as a potential trigger. If it didn't work, I agreed to consider trying the tablets. Although I was hell-bent on achieving this naturally, my tiredness weighed heavily upon my motivation.

I couldn't remember dozing off. I never did – unless I was amidst the certainty of a sleep paralysis episode. Although I was not entirely coherent at this stage, I knew to be somewhere between wakeful consciousness and deep sleep. Something I once read was due to neurotransmitters switching off as we enter the dream state. I began to panic and attempted to wake up; the feeling of pending sleep paralysis always felt too intense to handle. The more I struggled, the worse it appeared to get. Trepidation began to set in, and I noticed the room above where I lay swelling towards me, its unseen force beckoning me upwards. Recognising that my natural defences were fighting the abnormal disturbance and that I would eventually awaken, I slowed down my breathing to remain in the moment for as long as possible.

From the corner of my eyes, I observed a flicker of movement. I identified it as the faint outline of a tall figure just out of focus. Continuing to regulate my oxygen intake, I allowed this interpretation of my imagination to observe me. This projected manifestation of all the rage and anxiety Jason

Thomas had put me through. I ignored that I couldn't see Jack as I tried to subdue my defences.

As I relaxed, my senses fled inside of me, bypassing my body's transfer to sleep. It was a perception of travelling deep into the very fibres of my soul and, simultaneously, a sense of being further away from human limitations. I wondered for a moment if this was similar to experiencing what happens as we die. Could we retain that inner consciousness just before our last breath? Would we then have access to witness what lay beyond the scope of our reality?

As my body finally began to succumb to this coherence relaxation, the black cloak behind my eyelids reduced in density. By breathing out slowly and inhaling only a tiny amount, I gained a degree of momentum, managing to wriggle further forward with each breath. It occurred to me that my breathing somehow controlled the density of the blackness, which dissipated gradually until I was flying above the same barren landscape from my adolescent episodes. Familiar tunnels appeared below me, which I knew would lead me along the particular network I used when distancing myself from the noises that worried me as a child. It was as if the journey was hard-wired into my brain, which had evolved to acknowledge every thread of this void usually hidden from the constraints of a normalised perception. A powerful compulsion drew me forwards and down in an arc towards an opening in the ground.

Next, I was within the matrix of tunnels, burrowing through them at a dizzying speed as a bright light approached in the distance. Fighting the inherent and maturing urge to turn around and wake up, I allowed myself to sink deeper into the abyss and towards the light which beckoned me onwards.

As that light finally consumed me, all resistance disappeared, and an inexplicable influence took over my movements. Silence constricted the world as I floated up and away from where I lay. Above me, the ceiling bulged into convex and concave semi-domes to indicate the direction of my ascent.

When I was younger, no matter how intense the *pulling* sensation was, my instinct was always to deny access to wherever I was heading. As soon as I tuned in to this forgotten reflex, the moment collapsed, releasing me from its influence. A frozen disquiet gripped hold of me, engulfing me in a flash of terror and forcing me to retreat. In an instant, I was back to my physical actuality.

I opened my eyes to the sight of Jack asleep on the sofa. Leaving him to rest, I walked to the counter and recharged the coffee machine. Was that *real*? It had undoubtedly felt authentic, just like it had all those years ago. It was unusually light outside, and even though I knew to be awake, an emotional hangover lingered from that experience. It was as if I had only partially recovered my sense of existence. Something else had followed me out. I imagined at the time for this to simply be a connection to the encounter—a residual strand of unseen matter which I would follow next time.

Nonetheless, when Jack woke up, I decided to try those drugs.

CHAPTER 6

The effect of the drugs must have inhibited any previous apprehension I exuded. It took several hours for them to have any noticeable impact, and initially it was minimal. But when I closed my eyes, my body began to tingle, starting on the soles of my feet, along the tunnels of my nerve sheath, and into my brain with a flash of light.

It all seemed to happen instantly, and I do not even remember if I travelled through the blackness or even into the tunnels from before. Maybe the drugs had unlocked any residual resistance to this transfer, allowing my mind to be drawn towards the fissures of this hidden void without any reflex intervention. In a literal blink of an eye, I was floating through the air above my body. The ceiling stretched away in a bubble as I neared, then dropped through me, bending and flexing obscurely, returning to its original position with me on the other side.

Once outside my apartment, I was instantaneously in the sky overlooking the buildings below. I wondered for a moment why I hadn't come through the floor above mine but recalled Jack's insistence to survey the area. That I couldn't connect to a place I hadn't had prior vantage of unless, of course, part of its weave detected me in the shadows and attempted to ensnare me. As I had never seen the apartment above mine, it made sense that it didn't serve me any purpose. I glided forward and was soon above the park. The tops of the trees glowed from the lamps underneath, but each light flickered out abruptly as I passed over them. Picking up speed, I was soon above where Jack and I had got the taxi to Jason's flat. I allowed an overpowering sense of pending gratification to wash over me, which offered me a complete readiness to inflict my revenge.

I had expected to perceive a heightened state of awareness, but instead, everything around me had simply frozen in time. It was like floating underwater wearing a diving mask, halfway submerged as you scrutinised the world below. No breeze touched my skin as I flew, nor did any air enter my lungs. Whilst in this condition, I required no sustenance or feedback from my surroundings. I did, however, ascertain a fluorescent tunnel of blue light directly on the ground a hundred metres below. It followed the path underneath the trees, out of the park and curved onto the main road. I understood its influence to be guiding me to my destination.

Moving swiftly from street to street, I noted an absence of any living entity on the roads below me. I was alone on my pathway to retribution, and it was as if I was only seeing what I needed to see. All that mattered was the glowing blue tunnel, which I knew would guide me to Jason's residence.

I could faintly discern a high-pitched noise, which got louder as I neared my destination. My nerves began to sensitise, but the confidence that I would be able to stop at any time kept me going. Moreover, I had an incensed gathering of palpable rage that grew in response to my vengeful plight. By flexing and expanding this obscure but pliable substance, I seemed to be able to manipulate the space immediately around me, where my limbs should typically be.

I didn't slow down my pace as I entered the air space above the three derelict buildings, the centre of which was home to the tormentor of my youth. Instead, I descended over the particular flat highlighted by the gleaming blue tunnel of light below. I swept down and moved seamlessly into Jason's room, entering through the side of the building. The walls stretched away from me like a bubble, then vibrated back on themselves as I found myself floating just underneath the ceiling above Jason's bed. He lay below me with stretched eyes, and I at once recognised him to be paralysed.

A formidable level of power filled me as I watched him fight pitifully against the unseen restraints committing him to where he lay. I even allowed him to struggle below in blind hysteria in response to the profound fear I knew to be searing through the very strands of his existence.

A position I had been in countless times.

My childhood bully was, at that moment, nothing more than a pathetic worm. His perception was unable to comprehend the terrifying certainty before him. That something was there to release him from his cursed existence. Vengeance to be exacted by someone he had wronged so terribly that there would be no limits to his suffering.

An intoxicating sense of pleasure possessed me as I watched Jason squirm in terror, his eyes so wide I was surprised their sockets didn't rip. The once almighty Jason Thomas was now helpless to my domination, under my complete control. Trapped in an unexplored nature upon which subtleties of thought were wasted.

My mind blazed with memories of the years of torture he had subjected me to. This injected me with the rage I used to control and manipulate my invisible appendages to prod at him. At first, I went gently with my efforts, soaking in the pleasure leaking from the panic etched all over Jason's face. Next, I started to work more intensely, applying more pressure to my strikes. My intoxication for this retribution became so intense that I stretched my mouth, gaping wide to scream at my victim. I did not hear my war cry, but Jason did. Whatever sound filled his ears caused tears to flow down an aghast expression. I tore back the covers to reveal his emaciated drug-afflicted form.

I projected another scream at him, a cry of satisfaction at the sight of his soiled bedsheets and a growing damp patch underneath his wretched form. I felt a strange exhale of excitement coming from my physical body back in my flat, which caused my current manifestation to project upwards to the ceiling. I cried out in astonishment at this setback but managed to regain control and flurried back toward Jason.

I wasn't finished yet.

Without a scream this time, I lunged toward him and used access to my pent-up desire for retribution to start crushing his entire body. It occurred to me that at that moment, I had no resistance to fight against. My efforts were unmatched. Besides using his eyes to beg for mercy, Jason had no answer to my punishment. The power I wielded maddened me, and I continued to engulf him in a murderous frenzy, compressing every joint and muscle impossibly tight as they crunched and tore in response to my aggression. A sense of touch returned to me for a moment as his organs worked hard against my force to function. But one by one, I shut them down and felt their juices explode underneath my unrelenting assault. I sensed his bewildered and shocked disposition before he uttered a final tormented groan.

Jason Thomas lay below me, broken and lifeless.

Before I could bathe amongst the fruits of my labour, I found myself hurtling backwards along the blue tunnel of light at a dizzying speed in one accelerated motion. Mere seconds later, I opened my eyes again into physical consciousness.

For how long I was gone, or how long I lay there afterwards, I do not know. It was Jack's voice that welcomed me back.

"So – is it done?"

Jack's expectant gaze was fixed on me intently.

"How long was I gone?"

"Not even ten minutes – Is it done?"

Jack pronounced his words bitterly. His expression was pained, and his pallid skin was stripped of colour, almost luminescent in the poorly lit room. Something about his temperament was off and betrayed more intense anxiety than I had previously observed.

"It's done."

Relaying every detail to Jack, I couldn't help but notice how much my demeanour had altered. I spoke with unfamiliar but sincere confidence, even though the whole event was somewhat surreal. I had no conscious remorse for my actions; dare I say it, I felt revitalised. Jack's manner projected a unique aura of relief as though a huge burden had been lifted from his narrow shoulders. I had to reassure him several times that my recollection was accurate, but once he was content, he gathered up his belongings before heading towards my front door. His desire for a swift retreat didn't bother me at first. I was still high on the fumes of my exacted revenge to notice anything other than a tremendous relief at putting all this madness behind me.

Jack stopped just before he opened the door but didn't turn when he spoke.

"Remember the *Etch a Sketch*?"

My fried brain took a few moments to muster up a response. But then, a flicker of memory bled into my awareness. It was the last time Jack and I had messed about with sleep paralysis. He had written a message on his *Etch a Sketch*, before placing it on his cupboard top. The theory was that I would be able to prove the sincerity of my OBE by relaying that message.

"Yeah, I remember; we never did get around to proving anything was real, did we?"

Jack shrugged his shoulders, remaining with his back to me. Something about this recollection bothered me.

"You never asked me what message I wrote for you. You know, since we failed."

It was a strange interaction, and I didn't understand Jack's angle at the time. He turned to me one last time and offered a broken half-smile as he shared the words he had written all those years ago. Words that caused an unexpected shudder to pass through the coils of my gut.

"See You Later".

With that, Jack quickly set off, leaving me alone to watch the sunrise over the city again. The city above, which I had recently wandered through as though a god.

I spent the rest of the morning scrutinising the TV and the internet, expecting to hear news of Jason, but I was not overly surprised when nothing had yet been announced. He was merely a wasteful junkie, and his death wouldn't probably make the news anyhow. Maybe he hadn't even been found yet. Either way, I didn't care and took great pleasure in the fact that I had won.

As I was clearing up, I noticed that Jack hadn't bothered to take the leftover tablets, which were inside a plastic bag on the table. Underneath the bag was a sealed envelope. No one's name was on the envelope, so I placed it with the tablets on my kitchen table.

I presumed Jack would grab them the next time he came over.

Later on that afternoon, I headed into town intending to pick up some shopping and grab a bite to eat. Any previous sense of apprehension about interacting with the bustling rush of society had been alleviated since my recent venture. My anticipation for a taste of my new life granted me a sense of purpose, and I walked through the streets with confidence and verve, eager to sample all that I once avoided. After a while, the world around me turned into a blur of shops, passing traffic and unfamiliar faces; noticing my excitement levels starting to wane, I decided to retire outside a coffee shop I had walked by on several occasions for a spot of people-watching.

Nuts about coffee was a great place to sit and take in the last few rays of the sun. I contemplated all that had happened and allowed the events to run through my consciousness undisturbed. The suppressing shadow that had loomed over me, in the apparent shape of the memory of Jason Thomas, appeared not to be present anymore. I felt reinvigorated.

Reborn.

This was day one of my reconnection with society, and plans for the future began to dance around on the surface of these uncharted waters. Perhaps I would try and get closer to my old friends once again. Maybe their other halves could even introduce me to some single women they knew. I had always eluded further interactions with the guys other than our annual catch-ups. Nor had I met their new partners or any of their new friends or work associates. It was enough for me to bask in the shade of their normality during that one night each year and be reminded of what my life could have resembled. And if I hadn't, I would have probably become lost in my singular prison without the promise of any light bleeding in. It is without irony that they provided me with another strand of motivation I needed to carry out Jack's plan, a wish to see the reflection of their worlds when I looked into my mirror.

The floor was warm underneath my feet, and my heartrate burned with enthusiasm at the prospect of a new chapter in my life. A revitalising and comforting smell of freshly ground coffee filled the air to meet the calming jazz music from the coffee shop radio.

But my newfound sense of normality was to be very much short-lived.

Whilst watching a young couple amidst a domestic argument across the road, I was drawn to a dark hooded figure standing in an alleyway next to a row of bins. Its latency was more pronounced to me due to its lack of colour and absolute stillness, which stood out quite significantly from the immediate surroundings. People obliviously walked past it, going about their business, but it did not seem disturbed by the world around it. It merely stood deadly still and watched me from its unflinching position.

I looked away to try and reset my vision. I even tried rubbing my eyes to make it all go away. My mind searched for a beacon of hope, and my subsequent response was to blame the drugs in my system. But as I glanced back up, its gaunt frame leaned obscurely in my direction, not only noticing me but fixing on me, desperate to make its presence felt.

From its short distance away, I knew it to be abnormally tall. This eliminated it as being Jason Thomas and left me considering another possibility. One which froze my blood in an instant. A festering realisation crept up on me as I accepted my watcher for who he was.

A palpable sense of anguish accompanied this revelation.

No!

No, it couldn't be.

The frantic vibrations of the front door banging from my childhood stirred again within me, as did the river's pungent smell.

A spear of ice pierced my soul, and my mind raced and spun around, searching for any answer other than the certainty I now faced. In a brief moment of clarity, my thoughts wandered to the words of an article I had once read. It was about how it was proven that some people had been documented to faint if faced with a spectacle that was profoundly terrifying enough. Desperate for any kind of respite, I wished the same for myself at that moment. I even began to wish for death.

Beneath me, the ground swelled and relaxed as if trying to breathe me into its bowels. Balance failed me as I tried to stand. My dizzying mind spun in response to the adulterated atmosphere. An atmosphere thick with malice. As the world began to fold in and around me, it was as though nature itself was turning against me.

Without warning, as I watched in abject terror, that thing across the road moved slowly and deliberately towards me. Its motion was less human and comparable to a giant insect, but it moved with a singular purpose.

It was heading for me.

CHAPTER 7

I hurried through the park, desperate to gather some distance from my pursuer. A consuming sense of menace polluted the thickened atmosphere, which weighed on me like a heavy pressure. My feet became lead appendages in response to a suppressing force that made me struggle to maintain balance. A chilling sense of utter helplessness filled my heart as I began acknowledging who the entity was that approached.

 Light still hung in the sky, but every inch of the park seemed foreboding and deeply unsettled by something which stained its undertone. Even the slight breeze cutting through the trees was made up of unseen hands frantically reaching out to grab me. Once tall and silent, the trees now stood aggressive and menacing, swaying towards me from the forest canopy. The breeze did little to cool my warming skin, and the unexpected clouds above moved more quickly than usual, obscuring my balance further. My chest tightened, and I struggled to breathe the air that appeared to be starved of oxygen. But it was the look on people's faces that bothered me the most. The curious eyes of passing strangers observed me with sorrow from every angle. Their glowing orbs trained upon me as the air cracked and whooshed in front of me. And within that air clung a foul scent of decay which filled my lungs as tortured faces twisted aggressively towards me, threatening and looming.

I prayed for this feeling to be directly attributable to the drugs still in my system, but deep down inside, I knew who it was that now pursued me. A lifetime of memories shook through my mind, disorientating me further until the face of my old friend Jack flashed before my eyes. Pulling out my phone, I called his number, but it went straight to voicemail. Nature's attack on me gave me pause for a short respite as I remembered a previously unimportant detail.

The envelope.

With one final effort, I screamed and powered forward, managing to release myself from the hidden shackles that bound me. I continued through the park and raced over the bridge, the dull rhythm of my heart pounding all that was left of my recent ambush. Soon I was on my street, my lungs burning with the effort of my escape. Other than a dizzying pain in my skull, the world had stilled by the time I entered my apartment block. Glancing behind me as I went over the threshold, I saw the street was empty, but a sense of dread remained imprinted on reality which was somehow wrapping its sinewy fingers around my neck. A hot flush of nausea overcame me as I pondered just what was inside the envelope Jack had left behind.

I charged through my front door, locking it immediately behind me, ignoring the certainty that a physical barrier would do little to save me. Without pausing for a breath, I grabbed the envelope and ripped it open. Sweat dripped from my face and slightly obscured the words which looked to have been written by a child. Wiping my brow with a shaking hand, I quickly read through the note addressed to me, and my heart filled with ice as the words leapt out at me.

To my old friend,

Firstly, please accept my apology for what I have done. By the end of this letter and when you are visited later, you will hopefully understand why I had to resort to these measures.

Growing up, you were my best friend, and I loved you and the guys like brothers. But when I needed you the most, you weren't there. Especially when things got bad at home with my mum and the drugs, it was like I had become an inconvenience to you. All I wanted was someone to help me back then like I always did for you guys.

As I became that burden to you, I now need to return the favour, I am afraid. Please know that I had no choice in this, but it's time to share with you what I have carried alone for all these years.

Something real latched onto me after what happened with my stepdad. The same something that visited us both after what we did to Old Charlie. It was always there, to be honest, waiting for us to allow it access from wherever it festered.

I had always feared Old Charlie to be watching me from the shadows, and now there is no doubt. Ironically, Charlie offered me a way out of this nightmare. Charlie spent three days alive and alone while trying to reach out to us. He just wanted someone to save him, but we didn't listen to his cries. He has now evolved from exposure to whatever evil and vengeful creatures he has shared the darkness with. He wanted us both to suffer for what we did, but you somehow managed to keep him out.

During sleep paralysis, we are offered a glimpse of what lies behind the fabric of reality. Whether these monsters are fashioned by our own imaginations or whether the dead themselves walk these realms, I do not yet know. I can tell you, though, that astral projection is the key to opening the doorway to these monsters who are not meant to be disturbed.

Old Charlie offered me a proposal; he promised to leave me alone to enjoy my future if I led him to you. I know he will be there when my final breath eventually spills from my body, but this way, I get another shot at the life I have almost ruined. As I said, I have no choice but to agree to his offer. I urge you to see beyond my selfish act and can assure you there is much more to this. I didn't tell you this, but I have a girlfriend. She is fighting her demons whilst carrying my unborn child. Maybe now you can begin to appreciate my actions.

It's a deal with the devil, but there is no other option on the table, so I have had to take this gamble. I trust his words implicitly, as it's not like he hasn't had the opportunity to take me instead. Following me patiently for years, torturing me with his presence, but it was you he wanted all along. If you remember, you are the one who had the idea to jump out and scare him all those years ago by the river. I just went along with things…

Do not try and call me; I have destroyed my phone, and I will be long gone by the time you get this letter.

I am sorry, my old friend, and I hope you understand. I simply had no way out.

I dropped the letter and walked out onto my balcony. As I stared at the world in front of me, I searched the deepest recesses of my mind for an answer, but no solution other than the wish for all of this to be a bad dream presented itself. Beyond the darkening city, the distant hills that had acted as a beacon of change not so long ago now stood more pronounced than ever. In front of the mountains, the town was equally threatening. Each cloud-greyed building towered like erect spider legs, ready to capture any prey caught in their web. And downstairs, in front of the park, a tall figure watched me from across the road. Something half-human, half-monster. A hideous organism that had been dragged straight out of the grave. The air between us somehow stretched unnaturally under the waning sun's soft glow, causing me to feel dizzy and nauseous.

Draped in the rain-drenched and mud-covered jacket we had left him in, Old Charlie smiled at me with a blood-stained menacing sneer, his skin a deathly shade of pale, his clothing covered in dust. I identified deep dark sockets that watched me, and I became lost in his gaze as he reached out to me. This abomination then pointed at me before vanishing in front of my eyes. At that moment, I prayed desperately to a god I didn't have faith in for any scraps of salvation but knew my demands to be unheard.

The sound of vibrating drew me back inside. I quickly picked up my mobile to see several messages from the guys telling me to make contact and that Jack had been found dead on a train to Carlisle.

"Looks like Old Charlie never kept his side of the bargain with Jack then," I spoke to myself without any sense of remorse.

For the remainder of the evening, I drank myself into a stupor and paced anxiously back and forth from the balcony to my sofa. With the buzz of the alcohol stirring in my blood, I tried to regain a sense of hope and even believed for a moment that I would be able to desensitise myself, as I had done for many years. But deep within me, I knew there to be a wide-open door that I had no means of closing, and as the night drew on, I reluctantly began to make peace with this realisation.

As Jack had said, astral projection was the key to whatever lurked beyond our perceived reality. I had ventured further into this realm, granting access to the things that shouldn't be seen. And now, with the barrier torn away from the protective shroud of nature, I could no longer attain distance from the monsters that dwelled within. In search of gratification, I had all but invited Charlie to feast on me without mercy.

My broken mind was exhausted, but I simply could not allow myself to fall asleep. I took to the internet and searched firstly for Old Charlie, but happened upon nothing more than I already knew. I searched for Jason Thomas, and other than several newspaper clippings confirming his arrests and misdemeanours, there was nothing to confirm or deny his recent demise. Next, I filtered through case studies and recollections on sleep paralysis and astral projection, but the consensus seemed to be that this was an area of nonsense. This killed off any notion I had of contacting the authorities.

Like there was anything they or anyone else could do!

Drifting through a manufactured world of countless words and pictures, my body began to yield to the effects of the alcohol. Even though I swear to have only closed my eyes for a few seconds, it proved to be a few seconds too many. Powerless, I again hurtled through the tunnels and sutures hidden from reality, but this time I had no means of control over where they led me. Nor could I measure how long I spent wondering if I was merely dreaming or hopelessly venturing into insanity.

With my ruminations now organised, and as my recollection concludes, I wonder, without remission of hope, why I am still alive. I am uncertain how often I have slipped in and out of consciousness. I also cannot fathom whether these unseen monsters that pulse and vibrate against the fissures of reality are figments of insanity or something frightfully sincere. I do not have long to wait as the cold shudder of my torment returns with absolute certainty.

I abruptly awaken from my confusion to the terrible ear-shattering scream of something directly in front of me. My eyes open to the appalling image of Old Charlie, who floats inverted in the space above me, grinning at me from a rotten cavern stretching across his dreadful sneering face. His eyes are much darker than I remember. From his pale skin, moisture drips over my face, filling my nose and mouth with the taste of decaying teeth and rotten weeds. His expression is a portrait of pure malice, and his projected madness creeps deeply inside my soul's very fabric. The demon before me is more terrifying than anything I have ever conceived.

He slowly extends his long pale fingers and places his putrid and bloodied hands around my neck. Although slender, his hands are powerful enough to cease my ability to breathe. I choke on the god-awful fluid which fills my throat, and my body convulses violently against his unrelenting attack. The familiar noise of the dentist's drill returns, loud enough to pierce my eardrums as Charlie continues to squeeze the life out of me, his eyes glazing over as though drunk from the smells and scents of my fear. With the sweet mercy of death in sight, I make my peace as consciousness flees me, but before my mortality yields, Charlie grins at me and promptly releases his grip. The terrible substance within my throat violently rushes out with a choking and burning vomit, and I manage to take in just enough oxygen to sustain my waning existence. I blink my eyes to try and clean away the tears that flood them, to notice Charlie sliding away from me, leaving me paralysed to await whichever fate was about to consume me.

The pronounced chill in the air is stifling. My immediate surroundings are perverted to the nefarious energy of

Charlie's presence, whose eyes continue to fix upon me, lurking and watching—no doubt taking great pleasure in monitoring my suffering.

The smell of faeces and urine leaking from my tenderised flesh reminds me of the severity of the situation. The reality I am now accustomed to carries the certainty that I will lay here until the day of my reckoning. My body fails to obey my mind's will to move, and any attempt I offer to fight the paralysis is met with the threat of unclean monsters that promise to unleash an unbearable terror. They are poised and ready to be released from walls, which bend and stretch as if breathing in each element of my surroundings. Each terrible breath radiates more malevolence from a void I had once wandered through to exert my retribution.

Although I have not seen them yet, I can hear their petrifying melodies. Murderous and shrill, like countless souls arguing drunkenly and aggressively. Words dance on the surface of their bellowing symphony, but I cannot understand the language. But then I recognise some of the echoes stirring within the distorted reverberations. Echoes that were once sung out to me as a child. Terrible noises of all the things that I fled from as a child cowering under my blanket.

Dear god, I can feel them coming. Please don't let me see those monstrosities.

A sudden movent arrests my attention. Numerous lumps of an unknown origin are desperately attempting to burst through my walls. The bellowing lungs of the room seem ready to explode as the outline of innumerable shapes struggles beneath the veneer. I weep with desperation as the walls finally burst—a frantic dark sea of limbs flood through jagged tears in reality, like water flowing through a burst dam. How many there are, I cannot begin to estimate. Hundreds? Thousands?

Together they sing a hideous song as they contort and frolic without pause. Gurgling, Gargling. Scratching. Their raucous music could have been a storm of excited, anxious, hungry locusts. Whether I hold my eyes open or force my lids shut, it doesn't matter.

I cannot hide.

The punishment is much worse when my eyes are closed, as I can feel those things burrowing their way inside my mind, relentlessly trying to feast on the scraps of my very essence. My muscles tighten painfully to their touch, and vibrations from an unseen pounding structure viciously attack my bleeding eardrums. My breathless efforts fail to draw in enough oxygen from air that is potent with the scent of decay. Opening my mouth in helpless panic, I inhale deeply, flooding my throat this time with the writhing and angry textures of spoilt tissue and sharp bone. In reflex, I clamp my jaws shut to release a taste of metallic rot and faeces, which spills from their open wounds.

To describe these abominations in words is impossible. The only thing slightly human is their eyes which tear through their blank, expressionless faces—tormenting even themselves with their malformed features: no mouths, noses, arms or legs—wriggling underneath a terrible canvas of rotten and pink wrinkled meat.

Obscure appendages often rip from their worm-like, twitching, bulbous bodies as they reach forward, fighting over each other to get closer to me, to try and touch me. And sometimes, their skin breaks to show a blackness immediately before a hideous and garbled scream. But something was seemingly limiting their interactions with me as they were out of grasp from entirely consuming me, like starved pigs held back from ravishing a lifeless carcass.

The only continuity within this relentless onslaught is a familiar set of eyes fixed upon me, watching and indulging the whole ordeal. A shape I can just about distinguish:

standing behind the perplexing blanket of squirming, horrifying creatures.

My visitor.

An unexpected reflection accompanies the undeniable presence of Old Charlie. A distorted memory from a few nights ago. Josh, Shaun and Todd are laughing contently at the bar but turn to me sharply with faces emblazoned with pure malice. I only see them for a moment, but it is enough to offer another layer of torture to my lamented soul. Searching desperately to hold on to the withering fabric of reality, my panicking synapses connect to the loose strand of unseen matter which binds me to my friends, weaving me into their subconscious as a light to accompany me into the darkness. As stunned and chaotic as my mind was, it still held the desperate craving for any offering of light to bleed through with its promise of hope.

A rhythmic banging shakes the world around me, and a distorted voice bellows from deep within. Old Charlie speaks to me, but his words are unfathomable. A cacophony of dreadful and inhuman voices blends to form a petrifying chant. But a translation from the agonising sound is gathering within me, and the message I decipher condemns me to pray once more to a god I started believing in for any scrap of salvation.

I will not take your soul tonight; I will make you wait, just like you made me wait as my existence gave out by the river. For now, you will remain paralysed in this prison with the door open to all the things you were ever afraid of, waiting for my return. You may die of hopeless anticipation before then, but if not, you will see me as your saviour when I come for you. I expected to have a long wait for your flesh to be ready for the grave, but now I can finally show you the dominion I walk amongst...as a god.
See you later...

END

ABOUT THE AUTHOR

Daniel Lorn is a horror author from Glasgow, Scotland.

Daniel has been reading horror stories his whole life and is particularly interested in the work of Edgar Allen Poe, Charles L Grant, H.P. Lovecraft and M.R. James. Daniel is also a fan of classic and modern horror movies.

Daniel's debut release *'Obsession'* has a dark psychological horror tone, influenced by Poe's *'The Tell-Tale Heart'* and the mythical story of *'Oedipus'*. Daniel's second story, *'Pact'* was initially an unplanned practice venture but soon unfolded into something he was proud to release. Daniel also suffers from Sleep Paralysis, which has proven to be a considerable influence on *'See You Later'*.

Daniel has only taken up writing over the past few years and writes predominantly in his minimal free time. Writing is very much a hobby for Daniel, and due to that reason, he has decided to self-publish for now.

OTHER BOOKS BY THE AUTHOR

OBSESSION

"HAUNTING & BEAUTIFULLY WRITTEN"

"TRULY DISTURBING!"

"FANTASTIC STORY!"

"HONESTLY CHILLING!"

"BEAUTIFULLY TWISTED"

It had never occurred to me that so many forbidden and unimaginable desires lurked beyond the veil of existence. For years, I had suffered in ignorance of this revelation, allowing my forgotten appetites to rot away within the depths of my blood. Although blind within the darkness, these cravings desperately longed to be observed. But now they stirred. Now they danced gracefully on the surface of my sanity, having floated up from depths unexplored.

You can be assured that the words I speak about the unpredictable brutality of my nature are sincere. I also wish you to understand that I do not consider myself as mad. The following recollection may inspire you to open your eyes to the secrets I am now accustomed to. You may even share the same notions and illicit urges as I. We are all creatures of flesh, you see.

Follow me into the darkness, and I will share with you my story.

PACT

"TERRIFYINGLY EXCELLENT!"

"DELICIOUSLY GOOD!"

"FAST-PACED AND CREEPY!"

"LEFT ME QUITE SHAKEN"

"LORN IS A WORDSMITH"

Can you ever really know someone?

With his wife recently deceased, William has fallen into a spiral of depression and alcoholism. Memories haunt him when he is sober. Memories he struggles to contain, no matter how hard he tries. But there is something else that comes with those memories. Something which causes him to question his sanity. Something unwelcome and deeply terrifying.

FOLLOW THE AUTHOR

AUTHOR WEBSITE

https://daniellornhorror.co.uk

AMAZON

https://www.amazon.co.uk/Daniel-Lorn/e/B0B2K73N3N/ref=aufs_dp_fta_dsk

GOODREADS

https://www.goodreads.com/author/show/22586790.Daniel_Lorn

INSTAGRAM

https://www.instagram.com/daniel.lorn.horror

TWITTER

https://twitter.com/daniel_lorn

YOUTUBE

https://www.youtube.com/channel/UCQ916CUxl2Gk39rByL77-iQ

If you enjoyed this book, please consider leaving a review on Amazon or Goodreads.

Thank You!

Dan

Printed in Great Britain
by Amazon